Acclaim for

MARK LEYNER

"Reading [Leyner's] books is like watching a blend of 'Saturday Night Live' and 'Monty Python'; they have the energy and insouciance of high-risk, off-the-wall performance."
—*Washington Post*

"With a prose style blending near-hallucinatory self-exploration, gonzo journalism, hard-boiled detective fiction, existential despair and cyberpunk super-realism, novelist Mark Leyner has been likened to Franz Kafka on speed or Hunter Thompson on Valium."
—*Chicago Sun-Times*

"Most current fiction is as well made and exciting as floral wallpaper; but here is a writer willing to decorate the room with the contents of his own dynamited head."
—*Entertainment Weekly*

"Leyner is . . . the writer for the MTV Generation, the spiritual stepson of William Burroughs and Lenny Bruce, only with a high tech sheen."
—*Los Angeles Times*

"[Leyner's] contemporary Joycean, Hunter Thompson-on-who-knows-what, stream-of-consciousness sort of way . . . can be perverse without being pornographic, erotic in an almost surreal way . . . delightfully inventive."
—*The New York Times*

I Smell Esther Williams

MARK LEYNER

I Smell Esther Williams

AND OTHER STORIES

Vintage Contemporaries

VINTAGE BOOKS

A DIVISION OF RANDOM HOUSE, INC.

NEW YORK

FIRST VINTAGE CONTEMPORARIES EDITION, FEBRUARY 1995

Copyright © 1983 by Mark Leyner

All rights reserved under International and Pan-American Copyright
Conventions. Published in the United States by Vintage Books, a division
of Random House, Inc., New York, and simultaneously in Canada by
Random House of Canada Limited, Toronto. Originally published by the
Fiction Collective, Boulder, in 1983.

Grateful acknowledgment is made to the following magazines in which
some of these stories first appeared: *Chicago Review* for "Launch"; *After-thought Magazine* for "I'm Writing About Sally";
Mississippi Mud for "Connie and Lester" and
"Octogenarians Die in Crash"; and *Eat It Alive* for
"Pangs in the P.M." and "The Spin Cycle."

Library of Congress Cataloging-in-Publication Data

Leyner, Mark.
I smell Esther Williams : and other stories / Mark Leyner.
— 1st Vintage Contemporaries edition.
p. cm.
ISBN 0-679-75045-2
1. Humorous stories, American. I. Title.
PS3562.E99I2 1995
813'.54—dc20
94–31359
CIP

Manufactured in the United States of America
10 9 8 7 6 5 4 3 2 1

Contents

LAUNCH

I've given the raft with the woman you've been waiting for a little push so you should be receiving her any day now. She has a very deep cleavage like liz taylor. You may have to thaw her out. She is dead like I am.

I am doing my impersonation of the new jersey shore. I, of course, am lying on my side and masturbating into a bedpan that I've banged into a likeness of deep cleavage. If the costa rican nurse touches my nipple, I tell her that the nipple is the living room of a run-down two-family house by the sea. If she puts her eiderdown electron-image tubes to both my nipples and only if she shows me her shiny gold molars and sings Tengo Cabanga Por Mi Patria, I tell her that two escaped convicts from the woman's house of detention are in the living room, pulling taffy and watching a television show with the sound off, and if she brings me seconds for lunch when chicken fried steak is served, I pretend that they are snorting thick lines of crystal speed, and I promise her jewelry. If she draws a picture of what she thinks the raft woman's ass would look like projected on a drive-in movie screen without lifting her pencil from the paper, I open the living room door and mr. and mrs. hogan, a couple from philadelphia, enter and I pull her dress up over my head and we hypnotize each other and pretend that we have no control over what we say or do. If it is late at night, we pretend that we have lost the right to vote and that we have been sterilized by missionaries. We pretend that we have cut the moorings and let the raft drift away, that we are exiled on an island for savage morons.

The woman who I'm sending knows all about you. We have spent many nights reminiscing about you and laughing about your ingenuous kindnesses and social clumsiness. She is impressed by your poems and surmises that, as a child, you must have been force fed like farm poultry. Of course she is drifting very peaceably now right towards you. It's a fine sunny day. She and the raft look marvelous, rocking in the tide. She is doing her impersonation of an automobile show-room. You would enjoy it very much. She, of course, is lying on her back and the sun is glistening against all her automobiles, her sedans, her squared-off economy models, her red convertibles. If she draws a thin piece of kelp across the inner part of her thigh, like a bow across a violin string, you can hear all your favorite buddy holly songs. I, of course, am on my knees, peering through an antique vasco da gama spyglass, watching her revolve in momentary eddies. I too am enjoying her uncanny impersonation of an automobile show-room. If the nurse brings me a fat pungent smelling costa rican cigar, I pretend that I am a newspaper boy in a vintage 1930's style newspaper boy's cap. If she takes off her starched white nurse's cap, unfastens her bobby pins and lets her luxurious black tresses fall into my eyes, I enter the automobile show-room and yell, extra! extra! yeshiva boy slays showgirl whale swallows mob kingpin bald cure called hoax mets split! She in turn impersonates mrs. hogan. I think we want fifteen automobiles! she says, Look how fast my husband is! Mr. hogan runs from car to car spinning the plates he's balanced on each antenna. Of course she's drifting towards you now! She is coming to you of her own volition. Do not let that disturb you. It was, in large part, her idea. Oh, look. The raft has a nice teakwood desk. She is writing a letter. She will either put the letter in a bottle and throw it at me or save it for you. At the end of the letter, after recapitulating the ups and downs of her epically repressed life, she writes, p.s., I want the second movement of mozart's piano concerto in b flat major played at my funeral. She begins to lose weight. I enter a room where people are frantically pacing back and forth. Everyone thinks I look negro, I say. I am, of course, dying. I've placed two hundred dollars on furrowed brow in the sixth at aqueduct for you. She will be exhausted when she reaches you. She will be almost dead. My life is over. The nurse is doing her impersonation of an afternoon in bethesda, maryland. I pretend that I am a house. When she gives me a blowjob, I tell her that someone in the house is doing yoga exercises and that someone is painting the maid's room institution-green. The woman I'm sending you has taken off her bathing suit top. You will like her breasts very much. She is doing her famous impression of someone who takes three hours to eat a teaspoon of potato salad. The nurse says that mr. hogan is in a deep trance now. King me. Checkmate. Gin, he says. The bed is masquerading as the sauna at seton hall university. A young man named theo enters. Let's go down on each other, he says. My nurse is playing the role of a girl with very beautiful red pubic hair. You're not the most subtle guy in the world, she says. He bites her stomach. Yum! she says, Your whiskers are like porcupine quills. My father's pizzeria is the best in new jersey, he says. Oooooo! she says, You're clever, too! The costa rican nurse, who, admittedly, represents a repressed feral idealization of my mother, collapses to the floor and does her impersonation of a molting boa constrictor.

I am skipping smooth flattened stones in the direction of the drifting raft. I am trying to get the woman's attention. She is now a shape. A nude chiaroscuro set in relief against the horizon. I cup my hands and yell, I was sitting in the library when I first heard two members of the parnassian society whispering your name back and forth. Remember? There were only two books in the entire library that hadn't been taken out

—Portable Power Tools by leo macdonnell and.... The Penicillin Man by john rowland, she calls out to me. I begin to weep because she has remembered. There are some things, she calls out, that a woman never forgets. I pretend that the cliff rising above the dark water is a lovers' leap. We jump. She is doing her impersonation of a woman who has jumped before. The raft is disappearing now.

My life is over. It has been over for months now. I am sending this woman to you partly because we have preyed on each other's consciences far too long, and partly because you are my only friend and this is the woman you have been waiting for, for so many years. She is dead like I am. You too will be dead soon. When she arrives, do not mince words. Do not pretend with her.

UNTITLED

Stalking from place mat to place mat in a livid dudgeon. A voice skating beneath the exposed heat units, the new architecture of relationships with its freed russet scaffolding and its exigent separations, halves across the continent, elastic couples with gummy attenuating arms reaching across the midwest, different weathers.

Last night was my best lie, integrity peeled like an adhesive price tag. Then there was a violently styled adjudication, a kind of slapstick justice. A trial by pies.

You'll notice the foliage, the bus fumes, the heavy matronly arms reeling in the clothes-line of condoms. It's so Secaucuslike. So unreal. So unpleasant. It's impossible to prognosticate. The metastasis of feeling. The crossing of state lines. Apprehension finally.

It'll be nice seeing you again. What's passed. Tense is an inhalation that's held and finally released into a moment that is itself a darkening ember. The tub is filled with passing ships, a horizon of canary towels. A mirage of hips, a series of cosmopolitan glyphs, a brush that needs brushing. Strawberries springing from the tile's crevices where once only mouldy

grout festered, and the ample closet space filled with its magazines and its ideas.

It's three in the tire place across from the arena, lines of leaves
divide the street, the schools are emptying out, you're trying
on boots and saying something and thinking of momentous
things, the boots and boxes and stools and tissue paper, the
offal of staunch consumerism, stores are closing early today,
the proprietor plans on buying a can of fancy soup like oyster
stew and a magnum of wine, you're waiting for what, for who,
the proprietor holds the door for you, you walk past the tire
place and I knock against the glass, alerting squads of Cupids
in the arena's parapets, and the variety of twangs from their
released bowstrings is like a sudden diapason of desire, and
everything vanishes then but a feeling of regret about everything, the water cooler gurgles, lug wrenches and hubcaps
enter the ark, closing time is upon the tired place. Outside is
the world with its tremendous trap, that we ourselves, with
unflagging industry, have baited. We catch ourselves thinking
this way. Sitting nervously, thinking this way.

A BEDTIME STORY FOR

MY WIFE

The clock on the Hudson City Savings Bank billboard says
6:30, indicating nothing but the hands' exhaustion—it was so
thrilling five minutes ago & now that seems like another life,
when all the cars accelerated down Newark Avenue like
they'd lost their brakes and some of the passengers, some of
the women, craned their necks in the wind and their religious
medals pulled against their necks and were held rigid in the
draft of the wind and the dashboard saints bared their teeth to
this speed and the sky went vermillion and then purple and
then deep blue and then black like four blinks of the eye and
the clock's hands just fell limp... and you wondered who out
there was thinking of us, who in those houses, each with its
own private radio wave, each with its own esoteric policy and
testament, yellowing, friable, in some vanity case or hope
chest—who out there was sitting by their phone waiting for
our call, for our opinion on this evening that, like a kind of
curettage, had cleaned away all feeling for what preceded
it.... And here I am, bivouacked beneath the dangling plaster
of your family's ceiling, aghast in anticipation of their exoti-
cally emetic cuisine. The things that don't matter here
wouldn't matter anywhere unless the mattering was too too
basic to be located exclusively anywhere or here, I guess. But

what the fuck could that mean? There are photographs everywhere, (soldiers barbering each other in long elephant chains,
gowns and mortarboards, & a cabin and outboard in the
Adirondacks (?) circa '49, golf caps, sunbonnets, stubbly
white legs in bermuda shorts, fuchsia toenails)—and one
seems to say, drop your buggy whip, and the next, take up the
reins of finance. So how can a wistful harlequin in water color
or a walnut stock blunderbuss above a mantelpiece or the deep
suspicion that bridge is played here every week provide solu-
tions to problems that aren't even "interesting"? I bore myself
on this seat. Tedium is consumable but even its monotony
wears thin. Seventy-five percent of life won't go away; fifteen
percent of the time it has something to do with a dentist or a
deity; and above the din of the remaining ten percent we can
hear ourselves say, it's simply more exquisite to remember
having done the things than to work oneself into a lather doing
them—to illuminate our hats, than to requarry the emerald
mine.... (So we sat. And snacked. And they spoke.)....
What does your mother see through her eccentric pince-nez?
The atmospheric disturbance is insoluble and vast. A vast
plain that hangs in the air. And your sister. What could she see
in that bulvon with his indelible I-just-had-root-canal
face?.... My! Is this the miasma of a ruined abbey or the
passed wind of a mystery man or simple stink in vehement
affirmation? Or is this the fume of a cauterized bride that bites
at my nostril as it had that morn on the Portuguese Costa del
Sol to whose shore I fled when John Q. Nation gnashed its
moral pimento loaf of conscription vs. scramming? World full
of whack and silent discharge! Ah! Unmistakable prelude to
more of the same! (Is it Michelle who shaves her lap?) I quietly
collated several entries into conversation, discarding the
bloom of the family endive patch and the inability of Wallace
Simpson to wane in private for something topical, something
political. "There are a lot of wooden nickels in circulation," I
noted during a lull, revealing no partisan inclination.... And I
caught a glimpse of brother-in-law whose curt, eructed

expressions of disapproval were promptly reinterpreted by spouse or child and the combination of so much translation with this variety of baleful ogling made it all seem like the weigh-in for a Santo Domingan prize fight, and the clang of the dinner bell struck me as particularly apropros. Unaccustomed, as I was, to large families and their tendency to stampede, I found myself, perforce, left to seek the third floor bathroom, between whose dingy walls, the excavational capacities of a single light bulb had unearthed the wads of fungus, the tufts of phlegm and hair, and the clammy goop-covered potsherds that indicate an ancient and intractable civilization of slobs . . . but through whose window I can now observe the moon . . . the moon, the bilingual marquees, the fitful movement, the newspapers in the wind, Magda's pillowcase and girdle, the cantilevered window boxes of anemone and myrtle, and the bridge which gently spans the Hudson like an iron hammock. . . . I'm not of this clan. ''The raw turbot soaked in kirsch and fresh dill that you didn't have was out of this world.'' What do they mean—didn't have? I had it. And later: "Beattie and Iredell notwithstanding, Blair was the most fascinating, the most disturbing individual with whom I've ever been personally acquainted. 'There,' I can still picture him saying, (indicating with a hand over his heart some belief or another), 'we shall sit side by side upon life's long piano bench whilst you turn the pages and I render the most sublime strains and our souls, crowned with vine leaves, dance that rite of unyielding fidelity, and if ever the faintest bubble of adultery rises from my pipe, remove my appendix without ether.' '' The unfurled banner, the hail of trumpets: Smug and torpid husbands, (the call is collect, see?), I've come for your wives—your infinitely more interesting wives. Go back to your books. Oh! To kiss their mouths, under your noses. To feel their nipples swell between my lips, under your noses. To brush my cheek past the warm soft flesh of their navels, right under your noses. To lap the tart juices and meat of their veiny petals, right under your noses! Back to your texts, gentle husbands. To your fusty codex!.... "Buck is off to drill for oil...Bye Buck." "Bye Buck...so you'll be free for awhile?" "I feel weird without Buck," she said. "Forget your world of woes," I suggested, shaking spit from my horn, "Buck's a dick. He's no brother of mine."....And that woman, with her Ceylonese mask and paprika-dusted apron, draws on the blackboard which her admonitions invariably conjure before one's eyes, that "thin line between recreational gossip and basest schadenfreude"....Ah, danke schön, mother—but our neurotic ground sloths, Hansel and Gretel, have been locked in the Plymouth all afternoon and the windows are barely cracked and the vinyl must be broiling after two hours in the Dekalb Avenue sun....I can hear the mealworms gargling in the UPS truck that's burst into flames and flipped across the bright privet hedge that borders the lodge hall. The custodian, his thick tongue swathed in flypaper, peeks out from behind the venetian blinds. I can see the lodge hall without my glasses —it is so crisply focused—a kind of Valhalla made of dentures and prosthetic limbs....I reclarified, for your father, the circumstances behind our decision to marry: "See, me and my friends were out a few nights ago. We drunk about thirty bottles of Colt 45 each y'know and drove around for awhile, fucked some girls and vomited on them and we didn't say goodbye to them when we left either. We didn't have no jobs so....Then I choked one of my friends to death by stuffin gravel and dog shit down his throat while everybody kicked his balls in—it was a pisser—then when I got home my mother was suckin some dago's cock so I grabbed a beer and lied down on the couch and watched her for awhile—soon I crashed. I was dreamin a lot—mostly of fuckin girls or just rippin their shirts off and squeezin their tits and stuff—but then I had this real funny dream—your daughter's in white and everything—they're playin Here Comes the Bride—I'm puttin a ring on her finger—so I wake up and say to myself, it's time—marry her, man—it's a sign, y'know"....Ah, what is durable and authentic? Not gardens dug up to fill sandbags. Or barricades built of hatracks. Not the meadowlark's final bubble surfacing in a cask of Armagnac brandy. The world seems miniscule. A dolls' house. In lederhosen and tyrolean hats, we've ascended its stoop and crushed the Queen Anne furniture with our stupendous behinds. But you must return with me to assay the damage. We can wed our culpability this way. Wherever you go, you sense some wrongdoing that, like the imprint of a signet ring on the victim's temple, slowly vanishes under the inspector's magnifying glass. Then you feel your heart pounding once more and the hoofbeats of a blue ox seem to echo again throughout some hinterland you remember. Though perhaps nothing could ever seem as alien and as disquieting and as alluring as the sepia bluish-limned photographs of headhunters and tourniquets that one found in antique encyclopedias or as abiding in memory and dream as the severe glare of that attic patriarch with his ashen and bifurcated rabbinical beard.... I am less and less different from you, and you from that. Is this my way of saying—let's consolidate as a people? We are a people, you and I, whose history can only begin back there—day after day. And the pleasure will be retroactive—and vast.... So I said, get your coat on. Or you told me to put mine on. And put one sleeve at a time on! I'll try it on, I said. Then we argued. I couldn't even get the coat on—because the coat wasn't even mine. The sleeves were blocked up with old crusty tissues that an uncle of yours had squirreled away for a thousand years, but I capitulated because history teaches that every Napoleon has his Waterloo and here, in front of all these faces, was mine. I'm almost positive I heard someone say that I was a faggot who'd look better with an altarboy's surplice pulled over my head as I'm flagellated across the bare ass with a scourge of rats' tails and intestinal worms—but I may have imagined that. And I may have imagined this too, but I thought you said that I was a terrible lover, that I needed a map from the AAA to make love. And then I said, you're not marked by stately beauty, yourself. And you put a very flammable substance down the front of my trousers and I tried to represent words with frantic gestures & your relatives guessed Under The Volcano, The Carpetbaggers, Black Macho and the Myth of the Superwoman, Naked and Fiery Forms, No Time For Sergeants, and The Three Faces of Eve. And as quickly as it had erupted, the argument was no more. Though you've defoliated my tinea cruris for good, pet, our reserves for toll booths and road house vittles (a b.l.t. at the Pilgrim would suit me well) are bankrupt. But I love you. I love you. And I need you. And I'll never leave you.... And here we are. Now it is evening again. We are riding again. On mammoth steeds. Our outlines motionless in the chintz crepuscular moonlight, propped in tandem leaps across the vacant avenue and clock, like painted figurines. You look plump and pissed-off and I'm a little nauseous & the horses seem old and complacent and bored as if all was right, right on schedule and nothing beyond the horizon of this daily to and fro... the "excuse our citadel's appearance—we're recarpeting the parapets" sign looks perfect, mr. total's heirs are snug in their royal compound near Bernardsville, the nursery is quiet, where all conceits bear the imprint of the constellations, the pennant's locked up, the traitors headless, the throne reupholstered... there is the sound of transit but never the sensation of movement... the unknowable unnameable is vigilant.... but let's be honest, are we not flung from the earth as it spins—and is this not a kind of sleep? Ah!!

CONNIE AND LESTER

Connie and Lester are down by the well. Thick rolls of
toadstools spring from its walls like the powdered curls of a
colonial wig. Its floor is littered with shards and arrowheads.

I still have the taste of chicken livers in my mouth, Lester
says.

Kiss me with your teeth, Lester.

He steps back a few yards so as to get a running start.

Spinning stripes . . . make a circle, Lester says, waving his
towel like a lasso. He leaps at Connie, bowls her over, and
bites her calf.

Twice for luck, I say, and he clutches the other one like a
drumstick and bites it.

My ass is still stiff from Mass yesterday.

Lester pokes his thumb through the cellophane bag of pis-
tachio nuts, I love you more than anyone, he says.

In the density of limbs and foliage, veils of shadow and
oblong panes of sunlight partition the thicket into a thousand
pieces.

I think I'm coming down with something, Lester coughs.
He points to a stump of flowering moss. To a dragonfly.

The wind rustles the trees. Catch a falling leaf, Connie says,
making herself dizzy.

Lester's got a first rate brain, Connie says, he can do two-
thirds of nine without blinking and he's a great phone conver-
sationalist, she says, peering into the empty thermos, and
stepping on a yellow jacket.
Show them your tin cans and wire, Lester.

Don't be a stranger, Connie says tearfully, her arm lost to
the elbow in a crystal bowl of raisinettes.
Come out and see my car.
She puts her bathrobe on and steps across the yard.
There.
It looks like an egg.
See.
It smells new.
Listen to the engine, I say, turning the key.
It sounds like a poète-maudit destined to die in shame.
Don't, I say, handing her a tissue.
I think Lester really likes you, she says.
The ground shakes.
Tanks.
I'll tell him that . . .
No, look. You can see their turrets through the trees.
It's getting . . .
Don't, I say.

That night, the rebels begin shelling our village. Headlights fill the highway and rain splatters the windshields. Connie watches the windshield wipers and Lester listens to them hum until he slumps against a carton of canned goods and snores. Connie is ludicrously gorgeous in her pale wheat-colored maillot—her hair is chestnut brown, her eyes are fathomless. Lester too is ludicrously gorgeous in his pale wheat-colored maillot—his hair is chestnut brown, his eyes are closed. Connie counts one white line after another after another after another after another after another after another. There'll be plenty of time for tennis when we reach the island, Roz says, we should sign up for a court on Wednesday for Thursday and on Thursday for Friday and on Friday for Saturday and on Saturday for Sunday and on Sunday for Monday and on Monday for Tuesday. . . .

And on Tuesday for Wednesday? Lester asks, momentarily awake.

Go to the head of the class, Connie says. She unpeels her third banana, let's play a game—I'm thinking of a person . . . someone we all know.

Is it me? Lester asks.

Is it? I turn to Connie and break off a piece of her banana.

The road conditions and traffic have brought us to a virtual standstill.

A man unloading baskets, bags and livestock from the top of a bus gives us directions to a modest hotel.

Next day, at the tourist information kiosk in the bus station, we are told to follow a boy who will take us to the rental agent.

He has a creaky old red schwinn he rides every morning along the man-made inlets where people dock their catamarans and sunfish, where ducks in groups of three and four glide by, and he throws them pieces of Carr's Table Water Crackers which are the most popular crackers on the island, and these rides every morning before most people have arisen make him

tan and less burdened with a feeling of responsibility for the
heart attack his father had when he withdrew from law school
and moved in with two waiters/actors.

We take a room in a boarding house on Bonnet Monkey
Street. We can see through a hole into another room. Orange
and yellow balloons are strung on the walls. Ribbon is strung
from the light fixture and attached to something. It's orange
fluted ribbon. Don't, says a man, pouring soda into paper
cups. The woman lies on the couch wears fluffy blue slippers
reads the newspaper. Habit, says the man. The woman is
cleaning up paper plates. Some of the miniature plastic baskets
still have hershey bars and fruit candies in them. These she
collects. The woman leans back on a cushion she's put on the
floor and reads a thick novel.
> Lester: Look.
> Connie: Let's eat.
> Lester: When? Now?

The next night, I pack my suitcase.
Roz thanks me for having driven everyone to the island.
Connie and Lester are on the porch talking. They look par-
ticularly handsome this night.
Do you see that thing over there? Connie asks Lester.
I don't.
It looks like the thing you ate before.
I can't. I couldn't have, Lester says.
See that ceramic bulldog? Crouched by that basket of dried
reeds? Next to it? That's the head cardiologist at St. Barnabas.
I see them backwards. I have this kind of spatial
strephosymbolia.
Connie takes a rubber band off her wrist, and gathers her
chestnut brown hair into a ponytail and doubles the elastic
around it.

August will be over in five seconds, I say.
One.
(Close-up of Connie's face)
Two.
(Close-up of Lester's face)
Three.
(Close-up of Connie's face)
Four.
(Close-up of Lester's face)
Five.

Moonlight breaks across the embrasure of the window. The tide is out. Connie and Lester have waded almost three hundred feet from the beach, and they are only in to their waists.

TERRIBLE KINDNESSES

(with Nova Pilbeam and Derrick de Marney)

—May I take your coat, Miss Pilbeam?

—Yes, thank you Mr. de Marney.

—Please Miss Pilbeam, Derrick.

—...Derrick.

—Miss Pilbeam, I'd just like to say that I'm so terribly glad you could join us this evening. I know being thrust into the bosom of my family so suddenly must be terribly terribly bewildering and disconcerting, but they're a congenial lot and I'm so sure they'll take to you as I have, so be yourself and relax and I'm confident that you'll acquit yourself most admirably.... Why Miss Pilbeam, you're crying.

—No...it's just...

—Yes you are. What's the trouble dear, come come. Here, wipe your eyes with this and tell me what this is all about.

—Thank you, Derrick...it's...it's just that no one's ever been so...so kind to me before.

—Really?

—Yes. I...I was rather ill-treated as a child.

—Ill-treated? Why...let me get you a brandy, dear. How would that be?

—Oh thank you ever so kindly, Derrick...thank you ever... ever so kindly.

THE GLOVE
DEPARTMENT

Here we are again. A pulsing monotonous breathing of accordions. A confluence of dyes.

There is a kind of crystalline monumentality to the spots of peptides which lead like footprints down the forested mountainside to Lake Lugano where you have been brought by Sikorsky helicopter and I by Otis elevator, where a sprig of orange blossoms hovers weightlessly over your bosom, where penniless flâneurs and chess theoreticians in red berets writhe like storm clouds in this, the watery sector of the zodiac. There is a periodical wiping out of the impressions received on the visual projection cortex, but are you the anonymous friend who sent me a subscription to Ebony magazine on the anniversary of my hernia?

The sun is still, like a butterfly held in resin. The street is bordered by trees whose branches poke out like cocktail toothpicks. Listen. It sounds like the music a Russian would figure skate to. Sidewalk merchants sell boiled beets, chestnuts, and noodle soup, reason has been discarded in favor of ecstasy, and, like mice eating cheese in a cartoon, it registers deep in your mood ring. Like Napoleon, my pockets are stuffed with letters too foolish to send, but I have found aspects of your face among the brittle flakes of paint beneath this radiator, in tar pools of eolithic ax heads and stegadon bones, and in the frescoed boudoir of mr. and mrs. cork supplier. Here and there! Simpering like an organ grinder's monkey. But tonight the lentissimo rhythms of our smoldering frames will rub away the past because you are my pink eraser, my integer with no factor except yourself and one, and I am the mischievous kitten toying within your petticoats.

Here we are again, glued to the floor of a matinee, at the apiary, in the methedrine factory, in the lush breadfruit grove near Montego Bay where we curtsied like mechanical toys until dawn in a oceanfront cabana called the ancien-régime that was as accessible as Manhattan, that was like a display at Gimbels for swimwear, and even dummies have feelings, even marionettes complain of headaches, even porcelain geese have a vague sense of haplessness, even a glass of seltzer harbors a kind of festering "what if such and suchness", so however one audits the figures, they add up, and the sum is a snowballing of coy, timid indiscretions, of pot-valiant audacity, of jammed broadcasts, of inadvertent breaches of confidence, of bungled trysts, unscrupulous geisha girls, and mislabeled blood types, so here we are, mio dolce amore, at the homecoming it took chains to secure.

Before I go to the guillotine, I have one thing to say and though it may sound like it is a far far better thing I do than I have ever done, what I really mean is this, if your reserve of renewable energy sources dwindles dangerously low, burn these documents, this itinerary for dominoes, before you burn your bridge chairs, your diving board, your combustible scenery and if it annoys you, don't swallow hormones and jump out a window like some kind of new yorker; but when, out of the corner of your eye, you mistook the red kinney shoes sign for the sunset, and rush hour traffic for the rio grande, the shot glass shook in my hand, and now in the dining car the air is thick with the chalky debris of this wobbling orbit and the slightest pang feels isometric and giddy and wanton like so many handfuls of hair, because I have drawn asbestos dust into my lungs and drunk the milk of michigan and dragged you out of an impending marriage for twelve hours in plain night.

But now it's just evening and you are a cure for ulcers, so would it turn you on more if I spilled this mug of chicken and stars down the front of your blouse or if I took a job in Trenton and called you every morning at four o'clock panting like this ahh ahhh whack smash ahh ahhh whack smash or if I sprayed your lanky and girlish nakedness with insecticide and lapped it up like a cockroach languidly grooming its legs, because I'll do it darling, I'll do it you knock-kneed big-toothed rebecca of up-state new york, we can guzzle manischewitz concord grape and make it grand guignol style . . . just look around, we don't have much time, the night is a map with pins in it, the yokels are washing their children against rocks at the stream and refusing to send their laundry to public school.

Are you as weak as I am and do you need a drink or is this a foreign place more terrible because of its mysterious and regular occurrence or an empty savage custom bouncing a basket on its buttocks or are you trembling are you as weak as I am because here a river of fresh water runs out of the sea into a dark cavern because the fish have no color and breed in your pipes like eyes in the darkness and there is in those small piercing eyes an expression which no painter can render or because retroactively you are beginning to feel the advantages of steady self-denial and to experience the pleasures of property? I am not trembling because I don't know if the lips of your vagina are flesh or rouge and dough but are you trembling because I am trembling because I've been bathing with horns or rubbing clay into my wet yarn because like Dürer I have portrayed St. Michael fighting the dragon in a shower of diarrhea because I have used you without adequate ventilation?

Oh, night of the underprivileged whites. The noise of you gulping maalox woke me from a dream about soaking your sister-in-law in epsom salts and though your sister-in-law is not an intellectual at least she can pronounce her own name correctly, but to you, every eastern-european name is a kind of genito-urinary metaphor. You are fiercely heterosexual and well-formed, and it's no one's business that you've shrunk your parents and keep them in a terrarium, but you have a gatling gun for a mouth, and if that's a diary you're producing from your cleavage, I'm leaving. Who are you staring at—not that broad-shouldered svengali with soccer players do it better on his t-shirt? Could I interrupt your intratrachial injection of venom for a moment, or were you just going to the 7-11 for a slurpy in your crotchless suit of quills and steel-tipped espadrilles? Oh, if I could woo you for just a second, I would weaken you with blandishments and ply you with images of the soft life, of cucumber canapes and baked quince and firm Damson plums in port wine, of liveried chauffeurs and sandblasted gargoyles, of binding our neighbors in garlands of pigeons and searing them over bathtubs of blazing brandy, of ice-fishing in our quilted parkas with small bore pistols and geiger counters, and you're saying it, oh god your mouth is on my pussy, I'm making you say it as if it's a line on the teleprompter, oh god your mouth is on my pussy, and it's so terrifically fraudulent, it's so terrifically fraudulent—so much like mate in one move, like astroturf, like marzipan lungs, and this sensation of falling through a glass trampoline gives me an urgent hard-on.

You're a real woman, a kind of lusting dionysian midget-wrestler nymphomaniac who leaks like an idling chevy malibu, you're like game fowl, bark gum, venison, buffalo, you're like a beef cannoli. But there's a murderer in your station wagon, and his skull is a ballroom with a chorus girl inside, and his heart is a gnarled bladder, and tonight you will suffocate in the warmth of his yellow impetiginous cheeks, because he loves you, he loves you more than he loved the intoxicating breath of his orthodontist. Scrawled at his camp table, upon his map box, by the light of bivouac fires, his missives fill your postbox. Do you recognize his dueling scar? His silk taffeta briefs? He is the dimmest star in the punch and judy constellation and his message is this, don't be cruel.

Yesterday when you were an idea in my head, yesterday when I rode this monorail through the Alhambra and you were an idea in my head, the idea of you was like a hot coil that boiled the other ideas and it boiled the other ideas until they were limp and jejune, until they were mush, and my head was sodden like a warm sponge and I laid it against the window and stared at the thin snaking line that marked that hour between then and this irradiated archipelago and only then could I open my eyes and I was like a speech being sent from one city to another and the speech became clearer and clearer as you faded away and it was very cold and very accurate and I crumpled your stationery and blotted the beads of perspiration from my forehead.

When your life passes before your eyes, everything is seen in the context of its calibration. You see the hours as circles like the sweep of a clock's hands and you see the days as squares like the days on a calendar and the hours fill the days like little faces and each face is filled with its own frozen tableau. Are these the times you're talking about? Are you talking about the time that I slid my hand under your blouse and ran my knuckles up and down the ridges of your backbone? Are you talking about the time that you rubbed your palm against my erection and curled your fingers around my balls or the time that I pressed your breasts as close together as they would go? Are you talking about the time that you arched your back and moved slightly from side to side or the time that you caressed the tip of my penis with your moist fingers? Are you talking about the time that I rubbed the fabric of your underpants between the lips of your vagina? Are you talking about the time that I erupted like Krakatoa, and covered the entire earth with a dust cloud that darkened the skies for a week? Are you talking about the time I became so excited that the head of my cock just burst and you were left with a mouthful of blood? Why do you announce—yah, dis is nils pedersen speakin-when you answer the phone? You are not nils pedersen, although there are mornings when, naked save a sock and my wristwatch, I feel like peggy cass or ignatius of loyola, but

...those stills from our past are faded daguerreotypes, memories held together with brittle crumbling sutures, voice boxes faintly gurgling in jars of formaldehyde, and now while you blow another bubble of saliva and I sink my last quarter in this panty hose machine, the moon like a magnet has warped our silhouettes and you have given my last two cigarettes cute nicknames and plugged them into your ears.

I am the vacuum cleaner salesman in this orbiting suburb, the slumbering widower, the little colorful head on your pillow, the frightful shock in your drink, the fob chain, tobacco, and cuff link in your caddy, the cherub-shaped pastille who scents the air in your gangrenous salon, and you are so many lines of whimsical tripe embroidered up and down my ass, a tasteless remake of your mother who herself was a platter of luncheon meats.

So, before the surgeon takes ten paces and aims his laser at my knotted skull, before he addresses this malignant growth with his 7-iron and takes a swing or two, before he says grace and sinks his carving knife into the sinew and gristle of my brain, I have one thing to say and though it may sound like death be not proud though some have called thee mighty and dreadful, what I really mean is this, your sister is too self-conscious about her weight and that's why she had such a terrible time in Atlantic City. She never should have allowed that kind of silliness to dampen the pleasure of winning six thousand dollars. Now, suddenly, you seem thrilled that she's finally met someone, but look who she's invited into her life and inadvertently into yours—a man who's indicted each tuesday and thursday, a man who whiles his time away suborning witnesses and garroting jurors, and doesn't the thought of them making love in that squalid waterfront shack make it difficult for you to finish your spinach or is it somewhat exciting to imagine their rhythms amidst the ebb and flow of iridescent waters and the whirrr and thunk of flying cargo hooks? But I suppose you're right, someday they'll rope off his bathroom and charge admission, and there he'll be, like Spinoza grinding lenses in Rijnsburg, sticking his hand between two pieces of bread and taking a bite.

And instead of cutting two holes in your mask, you want me to describe this landscape for you. But how can I describe the clouds and the blue sky or the lagoon and its smell if I'm coming through the porch door and I hear a score that means curtains for my team on the radio? Out of habit I get a magazine and stare at her breasts, she lifts her arms like that. How can I reach her? By describing the clouds and the blue sky or the lagoon and its smell? What makes me leak the word "sleep" in a trail? It's wrong to think that every well-dressed chimp, every little-league shortstop, every four-foot lothario who steps off the escalator in Penn Station is a potential benefactor. But to describe how they hang themselves with their bow ties, wheezing into their dictaphones that one final valedictory letter... Ah! That you like. You're a delicious elixir, and you occupy my thoughts endlessly.

Is denver a real city or just your mother's address? Part of you is like a feather, but are you a glyph in the snow that gives off steam like the shanghai delight restaurant which hunches in the sleet on splayed arthropodic limbs and breathes vapor? No, you are more like a holiday that one leases. I love to miss you. I force myself to. It's like being tickled. And becoming helpless. It's like slipping on soap in the shower and waking up in a broderick crawford movie with bright orange hair and running mascara. It's like singing mexican army songs with a black checker caught in one's throat. It's like a dream that ends with you pounding on my back.

At this distance, semaphore or pantomime, even hawaiian dancing would be completely indecipherable. The affidavits have been shredded. "We Are Closed" signs are everywhere, and every key has been swallowed. That cloud that is creased like an onionskin seems to denature the moonlight and it indelibly stains the water, and when your shadow falls in my eyes, it stings so badly that I find the secretions of my own mouth indigestible. You no longer look like a camel when you sleep.

The sequence of presidents has been shuffled. The days of the week have been renamed. Our old brand of kerosene has been taken off the shelves. Our favorite programs have been cancelled. This is a glut of coincidences. And after all those months of "letting the pieces fall where they may," of playing in traffic, of divinity school, of bribing cops and cleaning up after circus animals, frame by frame, this epic for insomniacs has worked itself through the terrain, and, finally, the rails have crossed and mark this spot.

So here we are again. Crouched between a blade of grass and a bottle of gin. In a lair as black and warm as a nostril. And tonight, in a field of pollarded tree trunks, you'll unhook my yellow rain slicker and measure my biceps with calipers.

The sails are cold and palpable in the bent light, and so is the cosmonaut's tube of chicken kiev, so is your jawbone, so is the plaster cast of my dick, so is your wrecked corvette, and our spines are curled like fishhooks and nestled in the sand, and the wind whispers vermouth over the bay.

THE TAO OF BEING
WHITE

I dated a lot of Esteé Lauder girls and was a monster to a few of them, until the police-state blossomed and fashionable girls from all echelons of demi-monde found their brains afloat in dishes of formaldehyde. I kept my figure up—which more often than not required surgery. And often the surgery was quite primitive. Bed of leaves as operating table, machete moving in moonlight, strange birds whooping, humidity rike sauna, grunting in lieu of Mantovani. Sometime edge of blade make ablation, sometime numinous human spirit itself excise excrescent wrinkled fresh.

What if prick becomes so tiny after drinking radioactive milk from Japanese mother that one have to have social life, perdue, this way and that a'way? Screwing thick-thighed horsefly in a vestibule of my lazaretto overlooking a burg and the burg's water supply and overlooking the puddle of hairy turbid fly love-juice. (Here's funny part—I cannot find fly asshole to plug with finger during fly orgasm.)

If I take you into the sauna, little lover, you'll die. "Take me!" the fly says in my ear, "Let me space out tonight." Go down on me, I say, and it lights after a while on my teeny prick.

I lay in a pasture of flags, and troops and their brainless slatterns lay with me. Soon, as the sun fell into the side-pocket of night, I was coerced into cooking linguini verde. As they passed my steamy kettle, the girls winked at me, some hiked their skirts and blew kisses. I just kept cooking. The wonderful thing about what I was doing was that I deeply felt a dedication to my job. I remember thinking of my mother and how I must have annoyed her as she'd concoct mouthwatering dishes in a seeming jiffy. To digress for a second, and I truly mean this and don't hesitate to nail my colors to the mast; the United States is the greatest country in the world. I think people should want to join the Army. Why shouldn't the Army overtake the university in popularity? Shouldn't the G.I., the martyred moral-frontiersman, soon supplant the teaching assistant, the canting troglodytic don, as varsity champion? The purple heart displace the diploma? I think of beautiful America as a tall and lean woman in a crowded pedestrian mall. A breathtakingly stunning woman.

"Want to eat cock and pussy with a friend of mine?"

"No," she'd say, "Your friend should join a service organization or a bowling league. Meeting compatible members of the opposite sex right on the job is often the most natural and stress-free way to rekindle one's social life."

And she'd walk on with that majestic bearing.

A woman like that: I salute her.

The next day, oil was discovered in my study; I was meditating when a black geyser shot up into my ass from a crack in the floorboards—it was an enema fraught with success, I thought. "Mark! Mark! We're rich!" Mom came caterwauling and wiped me and taped the lucrative tissues to the refrigerator, for everyone to see what her son had done. When the accountant showed up, he said, "He's made a million." But the money didn't last—Mom absconded with the bundle and, after a few nights of sturm and drang, I urged the cops to bust her ass.

So I'd sit in a drugstore waiting for the little magazines to discover me . . . shot after shot of the wet stuff . . . and every somatic glyph, each pharmaceutical dish, each smooth veined pestle, each terrific thing, reminded me of you.

I think of your snappy haircut, your shoes, and of wanting to paint the Eiffel Tower ofay with the cold cream from your face.

HE HAD ONE OF THOSE AROOOOOOGA HORNS ON HIS CAR

for Elizabeth Ross

Aroooooga! Aroooooga!

"Carla, he's here!"

"I'll be right down!"

"What did you do with the laundry tickets—I've got to go by there later?"

Aroooooga! Aroooooga!

"What were you reading about Vilas?"

"What about Vilas?" she says, leafing through the paper.

The kitchen looks nice. It's suffused with the cheerful sunlight.

"The thing about Vilas... you just read it to me."

Aroooooga! Aroooooga!

"Oh, oh...'At last Vilas lunches on the clubhouse terrace'?"

"No." he says, wiping soft-boiled egg from his chin.

"This, 'Vilas passes jogging. He has planes to catch and no

time for conversation. He must be in Copenhagen tonight, and in Tokyo a few hours after that'?''
   ''Yeah...yeah.''

   Arooooooga! Arooooooga!

   ''Carla!!''
   ''I've got...'' The rest of her sentence can't be heard because of the dishwasher.
   ''What's wrong with the dishwasher?''
   ''I think something's caught in the blade.''
   ''What blade?''
   ''If you'd come over here and look you'd see what blade.''
   ''What's caught?''
   ''Probably one of those idiotic ceramic handled hors d'oeuvre knives I've told you a million times not to put in the dishwasher.''

   Arooooooga! Arooooooga!

   ''Does Carla know he's here?''
   ''You heard me screaming at her.''
   ''Maybe she doesn't know he's here.''
   ''I've been screaming at the top of my lungs.''
   ''Maybe she didn't hear you.''
   ''She answered...she said she'd be right down.''
   ''Maybe she just meant that in a routine way.''

   Arooooooga! Arooooooga!

   He almost knocks the salt and pepper shakers and the bottle of vitamins over, reaching for the ashtray.
   ''If you're going to the laundry, take the stuff I've got.''
   ''What stuff?''
   ''It's in a pile next to the hamper.''
   ''Do you want that velour thing cleaned?''

"No, leave it. I might want to wear it if I go help Norman with the car tonight."

"His Fiat?"

"No, Barbara's Malibu."

"What happened to it?"

"Steven had a little accident with it or something."

"Why can't he just..."

"The trunk's just jammed."

Aroooooga! Aroooooga!

"I think I hear her coming."

"Carla?!"

"Carla!" they both yell.

There are no pets in the house. At least none have ventured into the kitchen and one would imagine the smell of breakfast to be a pungent animal attractant.

"Where was Vilas going to be before Tokyo?"

Aroooooga! Aroooooga!

"What?"

"Where did it say Vilas was going to be before Tokyo?"

She leafs back through the paper, "Copenhagen."

"I knew something reminded me of Danny Kaye."

"What's that got to do with Danny Kaye?"

"He sang that song 'Wonderful Wonderful Copenhagen' in that film about Hans Christian Andersen."

"Norway seems like it would be nice."

"Copenhagen's Denmark."

"I know, I meant Norway."

Aroooooga! Aroooooga!

"Are you going to call Marilyn about the house this summer or should I?"

"This week's very bad for me," he says, lighting a True Menthol.

"What's so bad?"

"Busy. I've got that thing in Morris County coming to trial Thursday—Friday if we're lucky. And I've got that crazy business with your brother-in-law's doctor..."

"Carla only wants to come for half this summer if we go."

"It's up to her."

"I'll call then."

"Ask her about something closer to the beach this time."

"The other one wasn't that far."

"It was a twenty minute walk."

Arooooooga! Arooooooga!

"Carla!!" she yells.

He counts his change and yells too, "Carla!"

"What's she doing?"

"Is she in the bathroom?"

"She might be in there."

"Do you have quarters?"

"Wait...yeah. When Marilyn talked to..."

"I need quarters now for the lot. I owe them sixty cents from a few weeks ago anyway."

'You should park in the lot near your father's old store."

"That's a fifteen minute walk."

"Isn't it free?"

"It's not even so near that store—it's about two blocks... it's nearer to the Stanley than to the store."

"It's first come first serve anyway... you could see a movie on the way."

"They're all Spanish."

"You never took Spanish in..."

"There's no Spanish there now anyway—it's all Indian now."

"...there's Indonesian, Indian..."

"There's about eight Indian groceries."

"You should get me some curry."

"You can get curry at the supermarket—I bet it's cheaper."

"You think that would be cheap?"

"Cheaper."

"If it's cheaper here, no one would shop there, never mind open eight groceries."

"They live there—they shop there. It's got nothing to do with saving a few pennies. It's neighborhood stores . . ."

"If it's a few pennies, you could just as easily pick me up some things."

"Like what things?"

"Like curry powder."

"I'm not even parking near there. I owe the other lot about sixty cents so I have to go there anyway."

"I don't have time to fool with that anyway this week. We'll have franks tonight—on the grill or something . . . maybe just a cold salad. I have my hands full this week. I have about three months of late planning to do in one week . . ."

Aroooooga! Aroooooga!

"What are you doing?"

"Counting the months till July."

"On your fingers? It's three months."

"You don't even know when you're taking your month. How can I make any arrangements?"

"I told you . . . Make arrangements and I'll work around them."

"Alright then, I'll plan for July . . . and it's four months."

"What four months? There's a week and a half left this month."

"Two weeks—and if I have to put down a deposit or sign something, it matters."

"It doesn't matter. If there's a deposit—there's a deposit. But call me before you do anything."

"I thought Art's girl got married and left."

"She did."

"I thought she answered yesterday when I called."

"That must have been Susan."

"Who's Susan?"

"Susan's a new secretary."

"Whose?"

"No one's yet. We're getting one more girl and then rearranging the whole thing."

"You're not going to have Fran anymore?"

"No, no, Fran's staying with me."

"Who else left?"

"Frank Tarrant's girl."

"She already..."

"She didn't leave—she was fired. She was incompetent."

"How's your penis today?"

"Redder."

"All European men must have red penises then."

"If they wear tiny mesh underpants they have red penises."

"You said European..."

"I said European cut, not mesh frankfurter skins."

Aroooooooga! Aroooooooga!

She leaves and returns with a stack of magazines.

"What's that?" he says rubbing his eye.

"Cynthia..."

"My eye itches like crazy...Cynthia what?"

"Cynthia Hayden asked for these when I was done."

"Cynthia Hayden wants decorator magazines?"

"She asked for them when I was done so I said fine. Don't rub it—it's getting all red."

"Do we have any Visine?"

"No."

"Are you sure?"

"Positive. Why don't you rinse it a little with some cool water."

"It's alright."

"Did you see the picture of Carter with the Indian headdress?"

"Where?"

She folds the paper and hands it to him.

"What's that for?"

"It has something to do with that commercial where the Indian cries about pollution."

"He reminds me of Anthony Quinn at the end of 'Requiem For A Heavyweight.' "

"Is that . . . is that where Bogart does publicity for . . ."

"That's not 'Requiem . . .'"

"Let me finish."

"I know what you're talking about."

"What?"

"That's not 'Requiem For A Heavyweight.' That's 'The Harder They Fall.' Bogart's a sports writer and becomes a press agent for this mob's fighter stable . . . no, for this mob-owned giant South American fighter who can't fight. He's a giant dumb fighter—the 'Bull of the Pampas' or something—and they let him get slaughtered and don't pay him and he's got poor parents and everything and finally at the end Bogart pays him out of his own pocket and writes a big exposé with his wife leaning over the typewriter."

"Do you want a match?"

"No . . . wait . . . yeah, yeah—I thought I had one more in here."

She reaches into a drawer across from the table.

"Here."

He lights a True Menthol with a kitchen match.

"When you spoke to your father last, what did he say about your mother's surgery?"

"What about it?"

"Does she need it or not or what?"

"Probably. She's got an appointment this week or next week with a man in New York."

"With Larry's cousin?"

"Not Larry's cousin—with a gastroenterologist."

"At Mount Sinai?"

"Not at Mount Sinai—at his office."

"She's upset?"

"She's probably upset. It's not serious really."

"What do you mean it's not serious?"

"It's not serious—she'll probably need it done every once in a while from now on. It's annoying and uncomfortable—but it's not serious."

"What's serious to you?"

"A blood clot is serious, a broken hip is serious at her age, a heart attack is serious, a stroke..."

ANOTHER CITIZEN'S
HOLIDAY

Paige had again found herself in the position of defending her stout republicanism. When the call to evacuate came over the wireless, we were like breathless kewpie dolls waiting to get knocked over. In retrospect, I think some of us were ready to tickle and goose each other, or slide down the banister like banshees, or almost kill each other... anything. Our wraith of a monarch had gotten us out of one jam too many. A child's bib with scenes from a chiropractor's office on it was draped over the trophy you'd received from the figure salon, and, in the sense of no two snowflakes being exactly alike, the spectrum of smirks seemed infinite and optimism's things were taken from the guest room and heaped on a mattress of straw on the gatehouse's cellar floor from which, ten years ago, we had watched the Jets defeat Baltimore. Suddenly, the investment of libidinal energy appeared transparently premature. And night fell like a skydiving student with an incompetent instructor.

So it was regretful when frog-voiced Dr. Bim revealed supper's deceptive allure. "I don't care what people say! I'm sick of pretending and scheming!" And burst into the florid leitmotif of the chain Burger Rex that fell on flushed burning ears.

When he shot her a glance that was like the pulsar at the

heart of the Crab Nebula, her body slang translated into the "missing mass" needed to bind the universe and she squirmed in her seat like Laura says Clarence does. She seemed muddleheaded. You could picture untreated waste surging up her carotid arteries, coursing through the plexus of aqueducts in her brain. She possessed all the qualities of a carrier. And there hadn't been a shadow of doubt among us that she'd eventually beguile some eligible westerner with her ability to transmit vast quantities of data quickly and efficiently. She was, in this way, so much like the public—not issue oriented; and, in another way, so much like Moses—the apotheosis of style. Perhaps prosperity lay upon the far flung frontiers of the empire. There were ten thousand tons of gold in the Serra das Andorinhas to be had. Bim tapped the aspic mold of the Krupp munition plant with his teaspoon and watched it shake.

That ice-cold metal lozenge beat in his body, his demeanor not unlike a palindrome—identical coming and going. Natural history had never seemed less like a change of pace. My snaps cracked in the washer's mini-basket tub and the red fragrant spine sizzled up the flue—the suspected mass of frizzled hair between the teeth of plumbers everywhere caused a great deal of unacknowledgeable anticipation. It was impossible to decide whether to stay or go and the local crowd had arrayed itself on both sides of the controversy...they'd quarrel and then make-up, quarrel and then make-up, quarrel and then make-up, quarrel and then make-up, quarrel and then make-up, and their eyes would turn like little pairs of sequins from wristwatch to wristwatch as if the time of day were a poker hand that someone held. In the refrigerator's hum one could discern those unsettling lines from Edna Keeston's poem "Chafing Dish Dinner Is My Name-O": "...and exercise devices / developed by former Olympic athletes / girdle the planet."

I had exhausted my patience trying to reason with him. He'd claimed that I brought the snowy weather with me—that I'd come through Union Station, D.C.'s gargantuanistic ecclesiastical train station with contraband weather in my bags. She sat in front of a Titan heater and the rotating blade forced hot air against her cheeks. It felt hard in my pocket. Let's make a mistake we'll regret. Again I canvassed the neighborhood, with my masquerade and luggage—the sun gently tapered towards the corner of town. Again this sense of ethnicity, this sense of culpability, which, by day, surfaced like bubbles in beer, by nightfall was impossible to distinguish from the sidereal backdrop that exhausts bullets in its dense ultramarine. Footsteps were sloshy—sneakers filled with champagne. He's got a staple gun, someone yelled. He's stapling everyone's hat to his head—trying to bring it all back to the 1930's. J. Edgar Hoover—more effective when he and the gangsters he chased dressed alike. But it had all happened once too often. E-Street across from the FBI Building, a hamburger joint, boys with radios strapped like life support systems to their bodies. It started snowing. It started snowing again. From the window, this was not visible. A striped feather fell like a limp wrist from the wine bottle on its sill and the flying saucer was an astringent to the eyes.

God, it was beautiful and while some aliens disappear through the brackish surfaces of patio pools, change their names, and erect lawn ornaments towards which citizens in transit direct their heated comment, others cling to tradition, the women allowing the hair beneath their arms to grow until it tumbles to their elbows like hanging plants. A week before our birthdays, we turned restlessly in bed. Lay in our submarine. Swayed in the hammock in our submarine. Held our ankles and held our heads between our knees. I dreamt I was the plane's pilot and bombed the city. How I'd hold you in my mind. The amaranth of your face wafted in the day's crests and troughs. But it was no good. Smitty felt pressure from his mother's side of the family to marry only a girl who believed that the sun revolved around the earth. He felt pressure expand at his skull's seams and he had a bottle of Irish whiskey to drink. I stuck a finger into the St. Croix bric-a-brac. Good-bye saucer, alien, sub, pilot, hinged headache, whiskey, bric-a-brac, stuffed nose. Good-bye full bladder, cher ami.

I suspected that someday this message for you would be transmitted through the neutrino mail, and ease through the earth's core, emerging someday in your smallville, and slipping through the gold slot at the bottom of your door: Where did we go wrong? What roadsign, in the moonless night, through the murkiness of our tinted glass, did we misinterpret? Why didn't you say what you meant about your needs at a time when our levels of wholeness were originating in our being meaningfully instead of possessively involved in the feelings we mutually held but mutually refused to acknowledge on any terms other than our own respectively, as if by different treasure maps we could arrive at the same X-marks-the-spot in terms of us? Should we have sought professional counseling?

The cab driver retrieved a discolored rag from beneath his seat and stanched the steady trickle of blood from a wound above one eye that had been inflicted by the jagged tip of a teakwood-handled parasol belonging to his previous fare. The embassy flagpoles were empty. Certain types, I thought to myself, are utterly practical, in the tradition, for instance, of the pioneering test pilots who logged their flight data in pencil because ink would freeze at higher altitudes. As we neared the General Accounting Office, I glanced at my watch and yielded to a sudden impulse, directing the driver to undertake a slight detour. Call it hackneyed, call it sentimental, but I had to see the Tidal Basin just once more. And idling near its shore, I spied them: two entwined smartly-dressed saplings cooing like Nelson Eddy and Jeanette MacDonald beneath a naturally formed gazebo of Japanese cherry blossoms. "There," he said, waving up at the glorious canopy of inviolable American air space, "is where our thoughts are kept after we die." "The Washington Monument," she mumbled, "is a mammoth white french fry stretching towards the mouth of a celestial teenage presence," and he turned and turned and turned and the lights from the high rises along the Potomac trembled in the water.

The train was filled with spirits of the dead stained with the dross that hung in the air, not from New Jersey, but from its filthy neighboring states like Pennsylvania. The train was filled with a spirit of dandruff and with basketball players . . . with their portable lives. And passengers were employing tele-kinesis to get lunch rather than wait on line and the air was filled with slow moving sandwiches, but now and then an alarming biological clock-radio would spark a mini-disturbance. Then in Trenton, a girl named Polly sat next to me wearing white patent leather shoes with little straps and she peered at me as if I were the creditor-dodging dabbler in laudanum and abnormality from whom she had undoubtedly fled, but, in the unblemished light of thorough scrutiny, the resemblance apparently vanished, and when she got a big package of tootsie rolls out of a shiny little white purse, I dove for my cigarettes, almost surrendering to impulse once more, almost blurting out "this is the planet of escapes, let's you and I swallow the key and stay awhile," almost quoting the astronomer from *It Came From Outer Space*, " . . . this may be the biggest thing that ever happened," but I became nauseated by the confluent odors of tootsie roll and Prince Matchabelli, and in my pants my penis drooped like the long ash of a burning cigarette. And then we stopped in front of a large Johnson & Johnson plant to let cattle cross over the tracks. So beautiful. Through the plant's grounds ran a network of pseudo-Venetian canals filled with the most luxuriant lotions and powders for the delectation of both rail and automobile traffic. And shortly after we resumed our progress, I resumed my observation of the passing Jersey flora.

I arrived at my parents' winter home in time to see the LaConti Construction crew unload from its truck the nine-foot marble head from Daniel Chester French's statue "Neapolitan Fisherboy Listening To A Short-Wave Radio." In his desperation to find me a suitable birthday gift, Father had hired LaConti to decapitate the statue which was on loan to the Newark Museum from the National Gallery. I had always been very keen on French's work. My sister, on the other hand, had always been a gravity buff. "Father," I said, "what have you done? You've defaced a national treasure." Mother wrung her hands, "You test us and test us—holding your breath till you're blue—getting outa the car, into the car, outa the car— you drive us to it!" Father snapped a bulbous rubber nose into place, "Gotta split—G-men after us—take care of the firm, boy of mine." "What did you get Ruth?" I yelled after him. "Go see, she's in her room," he said, wrapping his arms around Mother's waist, their moped zipping down the drive- way. I dashed upstairs. There, suspended magnetically above her beanbag chair, was a specially annealed niobium cylinder. My sister was on the couch in the fond clutches of her fiancé who had a nearly two-dimensional head—it was the flattest head I'd ever seen—her sweater was bunched up around her neck and her unsnapped brassiere rested above her bare breasts like eyeglasses on someone's forehead. What a meshugena gift.... We all felt smaller and smaller in the coming days, which seemed shorter and shorter. And everything seemed diminished and fly-by-night.

Well, what is so new about Jersey? Or Mexico. Or England. What could be new in this multiplication of the present... in these bowdlerized translations from the rural? The good life, so called, is over, and that laugh we'd flexed hangs a bit flaccidly between our ears... we seem serious about wanting to outlive each other... and that may be the one source of all travel.

We are unhappy fleas, aren't we.

Well, if ever there was a rebuttal to marital felicity—they were it. He inevitably left the oven on and compared her Belgian waffles to old sanitary napkins and never saw to it that there were enough bulbs in the house, and she, as you could imagine, was not the easiest person in the world to get along with, but... listen to me.... I've been chattering away like a galley slave, and look at the hour. The sun is up, and it's time to let the greyhounds chase me round the track. Again.

MEMORIA IN AETERNA

Hoping that one last slug of warm Shlitz would give him the courage to finally say to Patty, "I love your breasts, the way one breast presses against the U of your sweatshirt, the way the other presses against the A, making the S a spot where a man could lay his head in peace," Oscar tipped his airline cup to his lips. But the words wouldn't come and god Oscar wanted to slip his hand under that shirt and feel her warm bare back and kiss her freckled nose. "This is where I get off," he said, crestfallen, squeezing past Patty's knees and ambling up the aisle to the door of the plane. "Bye," he waved sheepishly; and he jumped. As he fell through the air, he looked up towards Patty's window and Patty was frantically waving his parachute in her hand, yelling "Oskie, you forgot this!" Oscar's descent, being the shortest path between two points, was swift. He hit the ground with an awful thud. I was the first to reach him. "Oscar, buddy, ol' pal of mine, say a few syllables," I said. His eyes seemed a bit glazed. "Someone just hit me in the head with a pillow," he said. "Oscar, Oscar," I keened, "You're seven-eighths dead, you're all busted up like a ceramic Buddha dropped from the World Trade Center—do you have any last words?" I wet his lips with my italian ices. "All I ever wanted to do," he whispered, "was finish my novel . . . and drag a good Catholic girl through the mud a few times." "Ciao, old friend," I said. Randy, Normandi, Ray, Rachel, Wayne, and me—we'll never forget you.

THE YOUNG AMERICAN
POETS

The Japanese are an obnoxious people because they restrict the sale of American-made concentrated orange juice, but their endemic monster cinema makes our American-made psychological tragi-comedy seem like rewarmed tripe. Japanese women adulate young American men. Their jeans, their tough-guy posture, their gum-chewing delivery, their violent inability to sustain intercourse. Jan. 29, 1945: her name was Marianne Faithful and she was related to Alfred Dreyfus. She was exonerated when her nails were found barely incompatible with the murder weapon. When I returned, the body was back. Waists existed. Hips existed. There was a legginess that hadn't been seen in years (ankles suddenly *very* sexy). She wouldn't allow herself to get instant feedback—maybe she was enjoined by the Miracle Temple beneath the Mile High Stadium. ''The door for reconciliation is not closed,'' she lied, tightening the screws, as the plumbers from the Bahamas who'd taken the old Third Avenue E said ''O.K., take my wife,'' the other, ''O.K., please eat my daughter's remains.'' I stood in front of the louvered blinds. The way to a man's heart may be his stomach but the way to a woman's heart is her nose. If you really stink she'll recoil and if you start to stink, gradually or suddenly, she'll stop loving you and she won't even kiss you good-bye. A fair number of Dutch settlers kissed in the seventeenth century. Later, Washington would kiss his wife. Burns says that the freezing militiamen kissed to keep warm; that the kissing was ostensibly expedient or "contingent upon field conditions." Soon, after signing important declarations, statesmen congratulated each other with very formal kisses. I study Clint Eastwood at the Clint Eastwood Institute in Clint Eastwood, California and, later, off-campus, embrace the woman to whom I've shown my feelings, to whom I've exhibited my notion of feeling. Then, after making reference to the vivacity of a cloud up there, she drops below the surface of the earth and becomes, in terms of haute couture, "unnaturally plain." Tuesday morning I stepped into the sun; finally my friend Marianne Faithful had mercifully disengaged or unenveloped herself from her maritimey comforter which smelled like, god forbid, some baby had cheesed on it. The sun had given her garden a facial and she looked like a person who had gone to Tulane—I had never seen such an intractably bitchy glint. I glanced at my wallet and then ogled deeper—no money. No money—no razor blades, no books about photography, I thought at first. But then I ogled deepest into it. Never before had my wallet seemed girlish, but now it was empty and dark and *very* sexy. I've been wondering about the thunder we've been having. The apartment complex is having apoplexies over this thunder. Some say it's shifts in the layers of the zircon-belt, which girds the earth like a digital watch of doom. Some say the earth is shrinking—that we are a tenth the size we were an instant ago—that the universe exhausts itself in a series of hiccough-like contractions—that we are loitering in a minute and minuter lobby. In the future, the qualities that make for a fine waiter will perhaps be the most sought after. There will be a "Cadillac of Men"—a top-quality ideal towards which the young people will lean their shoulders. Then, the elegant, crackerjack, and ebullient, eloquent president of GE insinuates himself onto *our* dance floor, (into my mirror as I depilate my big beard), creating an epidemic of surprise that no one gets used to, and cleans out our fridge—consumes our soup and soap, and spews his yucky phlegm into Susan's open lingerie department. Someday, picnics will be forgotten. The very idea will lay interrred in wax museums and glass-encased exhibits. Or picnics will even become punishable offenses. For some, picnics require full course meals and linen cloths—for some, simply a rope, magazine and tissues. But all picnic people agree on one thing: *Look Out For Ants!* their famous esprit de corps can be maniacal and sarcastic in the dirtiest human way—unless you legitimately confront them, they will abuse you en masse, provided they are not preoccupied with their day to day drudgery, their sickening housework that involves, coincident with a blissful ethics of survival, a highly derivative arts and crafts. Marianne tortured her hair in front of the mirror—a coma was not her idea of "stepping out"; 10:58! isn't my toast ready yet? The toast lay jam-side up on the sunbaked thoroughfare—about it resounded the boots of a thousand workers. The peasants came to the capital, turned into beggars within a week and went to the church to die. Why do some women still want marriage when all most husbands want to do is have a nice day? Aren't women silly oddsmakers? As for eligible men: what about the thought of needing a ration book to get a dollop of sex a day from a stewardess or fashion model or during lunch hour on a magazine editor's couch? I remember being much younger, fellating my chauffeur Champion during a rush hour tie-up on the Zwieback Thruway as the sun says "sayonara young American boys, don't put morphine on a pedestal" and Champion says "Don't fellate me with gum in your mouth—you'll drool and it will harden in my pubic hair like stone—as stony as the undertaker's upper lip." "O.K. Champion," I say, "I won't try to fellate you and chew gum at the same time." In the wake of so many historians and biographers, June Rossbach Bingham said of U Thant, "he inhabits a glass tower but not an ivory one" always kissing and hugging and squeezing the Mrs. with undiminished vitality. June Bingham grew up in

New York, attended Vassar, married Jonathan B. Bingham and was graduated from Barnard. When Jonathan Bingham ran for Congress in 1964, she became engulfed by politics. My houseboy Champion has friends who had a long traditional marriage and turned it 180 degrees into a new, deeper, open, trusting friendship, and recently developed a humanistic counseling program in Brazil and their child, once threatened with no dessert when he wouldn't eat his spinach (overcooked and watery, no doubt), is today's gourmet, delighted to skip dessert as long as he's promised his risotto verde con spinaci—the leafy green of the spinach and the buttery mellowness of the rice bound together by melting threads of walnut-like Parmesan cheese. I called my mother to see what I should serve with that. She said that a cocktail made of morphine or heroin, usually cocaine, sometimes gin, sugar syrup and chlorpromazine syrup was used in Great Britain. "Barf!" Marianne choked when I told her, "I'm glad I'm American!" "Are you kidding?" I said, "Use of that mixture in the United States would violate narcotics law." She averted the suspicion of my eyes, somehow. Later I yelled to her, "Dear, I'm getting the portable heater and going down into the Hole for a while." Bruce Pesin is a perfect illustration of the brown-tongued, canting, third-rate, feckless academic. He is a discredit to our race—a shanda for the goyim. William Howard, Motorola's director of strategic operations, cringed as he entered the commissary and saw a circle of bachelors surrounding Ms. Eggnog like a brigadoon of phagocytes. "Isn't she a remarkable specimen?" "She certainly ain't no guy!" someone exploded. One of the most charming ceremonies in our culture is the family dinner at which it is decided that a child needs psychological help. The milkman was over and as soon as he left I called his office and told them that *he* ought to be locked up—under a microscope even a human scalp flake can look like a stylized Navaho rug...a lot of people thought we'd be looking through Field Marshall Rommel's goggles right now. "The hot water in my apartment takes a while getting hot so a few

days ago while I was waiting for it I was thinking about everything from auto racing to wax effigies." "I often do that. Can
you imagine—a little boy looking out at the world." "The
older you are, the better it seems." "Oy... you're making an
analogy with enology." "Do you want to have lunch this
week?" "I want to have an affair with you." "Oh... darling
... I want to have an affair with you too." "You do?... I want
to have an affair with you too... darling." Thursday, Feb. 2:
We Are Not Alone. Saturday, Feb. 4: in a darkened movie
theatre a male voice whispers, "Kiss me." A female voice
answers, "No... we are not alone." Here's something that
shouldn't be hushed up: condemnation of extramarital sexual
relations ran about 69 percent in 1973 and 72 percent in 1977.
In 1973, 25 percent of the response said that "there was no
right or wrong way to make money, only easy and hard," and
in 1976 the figure was 26 percent. I'm non grata at about nine
European casinos. I transferred my accounts from the Gunbar-
rel National Bank to the First National Bank and began court-
ing the constellations of fortune and went home and eradicated
my body stains with great brio and imagined myself in an
Hawaiian island's version of the roaring twenties. I sense in
the inspiration behind prohibition a bittersweet poignancy not
unlike the excruciating need, felt by some today, to have resi-
dent physicians in their households. Sweetheart, remember
playing gin rummy? Someone smelled a rat and socked me and
put me on queer street and, I swear to god, someone almost
had an hysterical pregnancy. You said, "Sweetheart... take
me out of here." Friday, Feb. 10: went to see Cocteau's *La
Belle et la Bête* with Doc, Blitzen, Sneezy, and Rachel. The
little stewardesses in back of us needed their psychic cellars
dredged. Many people equate splitting the atom with balkaniz-
ing the island of Japan. This is, in many ways, a good thing,
because it shows that people are not letting their thinking caps
molder in their closets—that they are not intellectually
agoraphobic. How can people be agoraphobic? I remember
my nanny glistening above the palisades, above the crenel-

lated ramparts, waxing her legs, surveying all the landscapes beyond her simple smelly provenance. Had she capitulated to agoraphobia's shifty and seductive "bargain", god knows what the total sum of her woes would have been. It would have taken a calculator to figure out. Tuesday, Feb. 14: I left the apartment to get a Valentine's Day gift. If I had a son, I wouldn't let him go to parties where dykes were marathon violent-kissing. Have a son . . . ha! . . . I can't even have plants with the lighting my apartment gets. We engender our young in the sewers, teach them to swim, hope à toute outrance (F., to the very utmost) that they persevere etc. etc. etc . . . the point is, they invariably dunk themselves like crullers (crullers with souls and feelings, though) in our mess. People should not love without respite — even people's love for Fred Allen's style of broadcasting eventually waned — and it's about time that the young American poets took Marianne Faithful off her pedestal. One night she could be like a statue — cold and beautiful. On another, she could be like a midnight snack on a Spanish galley, on another, like a radioactive mutant. A few nights ago she touched me as if she were blindfolded — as if it were a last cigarette. I was so mixed up about sex that night. If tears were worth money, my pillow would have been as rich as a Texas oil millionaire who'd just won a huge grant. In lieu of kidnapping, more and more young people are having children of their own. Mayonnaise gone bad can be lethal and I wonder if being a stewardess is the vaunted career it once was. Ms. Eggnog left me a note: "Dear Mark, Go fuck yourself. I can't stand it anymore. They're lulling us into a false sense of security about radioactivity." I began to suspect some sleight of hand involving the bonds my grandparents held in escrow. I sent the little money I had left to Charo. Last night was restless — complicated problems seemed to materialize out of thin air. I dreamt of a babysitter who appeared to have X-ray vision as he gazed into a cradle. "There was an ape living in a house on a hill, blanketed with weeds," he mentioned to the baby. "Then doctors told him he had but a year to live. The ape said, "Oh

Doctor, please put me to sleep now." The doctor said, "O.K. Drink this claret and listen to this boring tape." The sitter threw his wine in the baby's face, waking it from an unconscious sleep. The baby seemed almost extraterrestrial, holding her pajama top. "Quickly," she barked, "get me some cold water and a rag!" I passed around two rubber or golf balls for inspection. I applied a little bit of soap I had hidden under the table. I pressed the balls together. Because of the soap, they stuck together and "magically" balanced. Yesteday, as we were about to end our relationship, Marianne was crippled in an industrial accident, and I had to spend the rest of my life caring for her. Monumental hookups span the countryside; dirt roads ramify throughout the topography like varicose veins forming elaborate paraphs upon the ragamuffin arrangement of brassiere cup-sizes, and gals sell kisses on the fairgrounds, while youths languorously sip mare's milk—good motels are being built in the distance—no one speaks English—a significant minority of women have shaved heads—distant neighbors communicate with loudspeakers—trucks deliver milk to the various institutions—you are my wife—good-bye city life. I spent all afternoon on the sofa, putting on and taking off my deodorant, contemplating suicide, sitting in the breeze, putting on deodorant, taking deodorant off. The vice-presidency is the spare-tire on the automobile of government and, unfortunately, many cosmetics and toiletries are carcinogenic, so people are wearing yogurt masks. Rivers of hamster and gerbil blood apparently coursed through the backyard patios and barbecue pits of America, according to high school scientists who admitted to fads of "afternoon research." One kid, now a dinner pianist at New Jersey's Westwood Club, smiled and confessed, "We killed a lot of mice... a lot of mice." Ms. Eggnog: Your letter arrived by carrier pigeon... I didn't care for the letter but ate the pigeon. Describing two girls, I once said, "She is the pinnacle... she is the nadir." Little women make sharks in their briny commodes. I saw a tooth brush against my grave. I got a job at the gift and toy store and had to say to the owner, "Your work is good—but you want to be the Nadia Comanechi of poetry." There was an unexpected bummer on the shores of peppermint bay. She needed tampons and sent him for them. He used his razor and left it on the bathtub. He left the toilet lid up and she sat in the water.

BLUE DODGE

I knew it. I've been feeling like a fat pig, she says, looking down at the scale.

I'm going to open the shower curtain now and show you the horse I got.

He opens the shower curtain and the horse sticks his head out.

His name is Cote d'Azur.

Here have a carrot.

I'm sorry you brought up words that end with -facient. I can't think straight . . .

He bangs the soda machine.

Damn!

You shouldn't have gotten such a large bucket of fries— we'll never finish them.

I can't afford these repairs y'know.

She nods.

They both look under the hood.

There goes my between jobs vacation.

You'll have to work between jobs this time.

He fumbles for his keys.

Are you decent? he asks.

I was jerking off in the shower and I came before I was even hard.

There's a long stem running through the penis . . .

Let me help you with those, he says, taking the wok in his arms.

They get on the escalator. He's one step beneath her.

. . . well, she says, it's a long stem and if it gets a bubble in it you can just come like that, I guess.

They reach the top and look out across the panorama.

This is horse country. Liz Taylor rides here.

These shoes give me a blister.

She throws one across the hall.

He steps off the bus, into a puddle.

Where've you been?

I missed my stop, he says.

Well, you get something to drink, I'll serve the spaghetti.

I want mead, he laughs.

She leans over and he cups both her breasts in his hands.

That doesn't look like you.

It was taken four years ago. Here, let me see.

She gets up to pay the check.

Doesn't your father know anyone with pull?

Her voice trails away.

He snuffs out his cigarette and dries himself with her bathrobe.

What about substitute teaching?

He addresses another envelope.

Messrs. Bad and Worse.

He makes a fist and looks through it.

He squeezes his fist shut and she takes off her sunglasses and dives into the pool.

He gets on Cote d'Azur and rides away.

Everyone goes home.

He rides back.

Where'd everyone go? he says.

UNTITLED

Now, I'm the instructor. And a fucking good one! No lackey or flunky or major-domo, miss transparent thing. Look at those azalea—where a rumpled tabloid perches now—and tell me which members of parliament are homosexual. Look at the gardenia. And you said you loved me. What a grand and condescending gesture that was! Ain't that the beauty of it all, the metal globe filled with a rabbit's breath. In other words, You are the Institute. And I'm the instructor. No lackey or flunky. My mother left me. In a bowling ball bag. In the bullrushes. Of the Passaic. This is an eeeklogue. Your sister is internationally famous. She's got a shoulder spasm. She's got a leech under her tongue. And a steaming place between her legs. And she went for me. And I swooned. Literally. I lost all breath. Oh you sweet thing. You hot thing, I managed to gasp. She asked me if I liked to watch people leak. You mean urinate —take a leak? No, leak. Leak. Like a pail or a dam. Anywhere. Wherever you go. Eeeklogue comes from eclogue, a dialogue between shepherds. And eeek is from the comics. And eeeklogues are made of the nervous, desultory chatter that characterizes the lull of impending catastrophe. They fill balloons like talk in comics. They rise out of a stadium that many people make. The wind flattens Connie's skirt against her legs as she hops out and capers carelessly about the disinfectant silo.

How appalled you were when you got your sacks and paid your bill. How appalled you were when, amidst the flurry of gear-shift, clutch, and gas pedal, I buried my face in the silky pell-mell of your strawberry blondness. To return the gland to England. To prod her insides with this fragrant banderilla. The reviewing stands are trimmed with pennants and bunting . . . the maximum leader is photographed in shirtsleeves and gabardine slacks. This pillow is a map that smothers women. Spring is here. Why doesn't my heart go dancing?

I'M WRITING ABOUT SALLY

Interestingly enough, I starred in "South Pacific" for two years before negotiating oil rights with the Shah of Durani and then performing delicate eleventh-hour dermatological surgery upon Birgit Nilsson at the Gloucester County College Hospital in Sewell, New Jersey, and now I'm writing about Sally.

To 50% of you, that proportion which does not know me— that proportion of you to whom I am a total stranger, "Sally" shall refer to Rachel Horowitz my girl friend in actual life. To the other 49%, those of you who know me on a personal basis, through correspondence, those of you who are even familiar with me solely on the basis of telephone calls ("Hello, Baseline Toyota?" "No, you have the wrong number." "How's Wednesday look for a thousand mile check?" "Wednesday looks crowded. How's Friday for you?" "Super." "Bring a change of clothes.") "Sally" simply represents an obsessive gesture in the metalanguage of "naming," in other words, a kind of distant love—a real doll—a ghost with a winning smile, who I'd like to have visit me over the Columbus Day weekend—that's the weekend of the 8th.

Sonny Liston remodeled my nose in the fifth round in a Las Vegas ring.

I wrote a monograph on bubbles and then became the proprietor of a ginseng establishment and my best friend is some clam from Cheyenne.

Yesterday, the 13th of September, a conference was summoned to London to settle a new map of the Balkans. It became evident by lunchtime that Austria's prime object was to deny Serbia direct access to the Adriatic. And, of course, behind closed doors, Austrian ministers' jingoism waxed turgid in the grand huff and puff manner. The resolution of Austria to keep Serbia out of Albania was matched by the determination of Russia that the Serbs should be given this access to the sea. It was so silly! By 2:00 P.M. Europe was brought to the brink of war and by 2:30 P.M. war was averted. Like ad hoc big brothers, the Germans exercised a moderating influence over the Austrians, the English over the Russians. Hardly was the ink dry upon the settlement than acrimonious quarrels broke out among the very political "siblings" themselves. The ramshackle state of European stability reminds me of the state of Sally's furniture. The edge of her bedroom dresser is marred. The wicker is broken, and the vinyl worn on her dining-room chairs. The cushions are worn on her couch and plastic tubing in the welting is coming out of the corners. The legs on the dining room table are loose and need regluing.

Sally—

I don't know how to title these times—perhaps "The Contamination of Happiness" or "Bewildered, and Bereft of Funtimes" or maybe "Here Comes Hell Again!"—I miss you so much I want to have fits. There's no news—only a revolving span of drudgery and discontent—barely marked by the passing of the days which speed by with the swiftness of a buried ton. The people I meet might as well be on the moon. I keep thinking, and each time as another realization, what a wonderful superb person you are. I just want to be with you. Maybe this weekend I'll put the pen to a cheerier letter.

> All my love,
> *Mark*

The Boston Celtics put me on waivers when I manifested the stigmata of Christ—I couldn't shoot without discomfort. I'm an Irish raconteur and I entered the Story Fest in order to win enough cash to buy Sally some new furniture. As soon as the judge said "Go!" I had to render flies in three different ways:

"I'll teach you the abc's of dance," I said and Sally said, "We gotta get some zzz's" and I began to shimmy unavailed upon, but then, at the western portico, a head popped up and we both saw it, you know what I mean?—and we just knocked that expensive oeil-de-boeuf style window right out in our enthusiasm to intercept the mannerless guy.

"I am zee zinger who zings at Anthony's Abattoir Sur La Mer," he said, bowing crisply—and his back crackled.

"Perfect" I said, "Now we can certainly dance, see—he'll sing and we'll dance."

"Nix" Sally said, "Shall I hit the hay alone or will you join me?"

"Loosen up," I suggested, doing a few quick squats, nipping at her tail at each descent.

"I run tomorrow in The Big Stakes you randy lunk—lemme sleep."

Needless to say I did everything to keep her up including putting flies on her behind. I didn't go to the event the next day but ascertained via reliable source that she ran like molasses.

The next night after another scene, I vowed to sell her— "I'm through with horses," I adjured. I took a whore's bath, zipped over to the club and in the enthusiasm of my watershed pledge, I split a card in two, sideways, and burst about four thousand seven hundred balls in ten hours of continuous shooting.

I was a bit hard pressed as I approached the second way:

The guerillas are the fish—
the people are the sea . . .

"No, no!" the judge shouted, "You got the fly motif not the fish motif. Get lost and don't come back!"

With the sangfroid of an oyster on Sunday, I accepted the nonetheless unpalatable notion that I had been foiled. I suppose I'm really quite frightened of flies.

I vant to be as mysterious as a voman.

Dear Mao,
I hope the people in heaven are real together. If they're not, I know you're organizing them.

Sincerely,
Kathy

The workers in the old factory were laughing so much! Someone had just told the funniest joke! "A Yankee goes into a drugstore to buy condoms. 'I'll have a package of rubbers,' he says. The druggist takes them from the shelf, 'That'll be $3.50 with tax.' 'I don't want the ones with tacks,' the Yankee says, 'I want the ones that stay up by themselves!' "

"You know, you look too nice to be in a dump like this. What brought you here?"

"You're a queer one, you're young," she said. "Love brought me here."

She laughed, and the laugh was harsh with the hint of tears behind it. She threw back her head, and touched the rose in her black hair. She had a lot of hair.

—from *Confidential*
by Donald Henderson Clarke

You see me with my sunglasses and cigar at ringside—then in the morning—it's the 14th of September—I had bought a purple toothbrush to clean my tongue and imagine a voluptuous coed—a pouting libertine in men's pajamas—a girl paring her eyelashes with the scissors my father had used for his nose hairs—a Hoffritz scissors! Some cowboy told me an eastern scissors won't cut at this altitude . . . who do they take me for? Do they want to see me cry like Jackie Coogan in "Toyota Sally"?

(This section should be read like a Jewish Haggadah.)

I began to think of my employees as students—two of whom were intrigued by the image of a hypertrophic drummer beating upon a bus-like gong. The re-juxtaposition of words, that is, simply, the manipulation of language, from a position within the matrix of a consumer society, (such as U.S.A.), or from within the matrix of a draconian society (such as ours) is an analogous operation to one which I undertook a number of days ago and which I wish to render: I awoke on the morning of the 10th of September and divided my body up into square centimeters and upon each cm. applied a different cologne— in point of illustration, upon one nearly matted area beneath my pitching arm I daubed what is commerically known as "Canon & Common Law"—a fusty bouquet with the slightest hint of sherry and damp tweed; upon the raised demarcated square at the base of what Sean Michaels calls the "milch pimple" I applied the somewhat rousing fragrance of "Turkish Scimitar." At any rate, each of the thousands of square cms. was "bathed"—as it were, in like fashion. The experiment consisted of, procedurally, simply this: entering a full early-morning bus and evaluating the response, particularly the distaff response to, first, the cumulative effect of the odeur and secondly the particular effects of each "flesh-tag", as it was exposed to the air. I was at the time completely unaware of the fact that similar experiments conducted in

Quebec City under the aegis of the Canadian Royal Academy
had resulted inexplicably in epidemic-style outbreaks of (with
each affliction a drop of wine should be poured into the plate)
Bugger's Itch, Bilge Mouth, Fad Dieting, Listless Advertis-
ing, and infrequently, Ridiculous Judicial Appointments. The
bus rocked back and forth like a buoy and before I could
collate any substantial data a behemoth percussionist had set
his giant mallet upon the top of the bus and its metallic richness
resounded throughout Boulder calling all writers to work.
Boulder's a writer's town; its streets bespeak the tangled
strains of the raconteur's spiel. "Sally" I said to the girl sitting
next to me, "Is that my wallet you have? Do you have any
relatives with irritating habits? Is an olfactory art plausible?"
Just then we careened into the old factory—the place where
great literature is made—the place where many of the great
classics were written including, most recently, Thelma
Strabel's *Reap The Wild Wind* and my own "In Susan."

She insisted upon reading and re-reading "In Susan" and
talking technique.

She pointed to my nose. "Run into a hammerfish?" she
asked.

The next morning I wrote her a note:

> In response to your question—how well do we know Susan
> —it seems to me that the question should not be—how well do
> we know Susan vis-a-vis the notion of character qua character
> —but how well do we "know" Susan qua Susan—a question
> which synecdochically raises the corollary—how do we
> "know" "In Susan" qua "In Susan"—at which point, the
> word "know" seems to spasm like a fish out of water.
>
> I've recently begun a new tack . . . now I'm writing about the
> agent of my twenty-four hour-a-day anxiety. Listen closely. . .
> he's like a madman on the loose. His footsteps approach with
> each creak of of the floorboards above. I can hear his bell. He
> murmurs, "Sally's forgotten you . . ."

She lay in the sand with her scuba mask, snorkel, spear and flippers and I built, like the bowerbird, a chamber in which to woo her. To woo her hence. To woo her from the gloss of the page. I looked at the clock-radio, at the photograph of Sally upon the night-table and again at the photograph in the magazine. My laziness annoyed me—there were three matters which required my immediate attention: the unraveling of a blunderheaded confusion regarding my bank account, the acquisition of a New York Times and the purchase of Donald Henderson Clarke's newest volume entitled *Confidential*. I was especially anxious to see the size of the headline announcing the Kaiser's break with the Prussian Parliament. I called two of my students and told them to get right over with the new palanquin and take me to the bank, first of all!

I precipitated the disco wave by using a bat bone on a woman's ear as a sort of musical dildo. The song went like this:

I know I've said and done stupid and upsetting things in the past—but please believe me, I want to be with you always—I just want us to be together for good. I have absolutely no interest in any one else— that's simply the fact of it.   Uh-huh   Uh-huh!

I'm not going to talk about who should move where or stay where or anything like that—I just want to tell you that I hope in the coming weeks we can make some plans (be they present or future plans) to stay together and perhaps get married.   Uh-huh   Uh-huh!

I just want to know for sure that our relationship is permanent—because knowing that will make whatever separation there is more than bearable. I'll talk to you soon.

Ah . . . if only nuptials were Sally's bag. Perhaps she's too much of the whore.

The sheets smell like Sally. There's snow on the mountain already. Is Sally alive? Has she been driven to resort to cannibalism? Has she simply been driven to a resort—perhaps Steamboat Springs?

I attended, uninvited, a soirée in Louella Menzies' smoky trailer. Nothing had yet been served and during a lull I fairly burst out, "Did somebody say dinner was on? What is the conventional wisdom vis-a-vis dinner, because I need the sustenance to make way like a smitten red-man into each valley and canyon where I'll cup my hands to my mouth and call, 'Yoo-hoo . . . Sally . . . yooo-hooo!' "

OCTOGENARIANS DIE
IN CRASH

Close to the field of battle, they await an enemy coming from afar; at rest, an exhausted enemy; with well-fed troops, hungry ones. This is control of the physical factor.

What is called 'foreknowledge' cannot be elicited from spirits, nor from gods, nor by analogy with past events, nor from calculations. It must be obtained from men who know the enemy situation.

—SUN TZU

CHARACTERS

THE DAUPHIN

VERNON, the Dauphin's chamberlain

LUCAN

JUDY, who feasted on exotic bird's nests for days at a time and dressed her Pekingese puppies in vests made of costly imported fabrics

VIC PIANO, owner of SIT-Siemens electronics plant and Pirelli rubber factory; Lucan's ideal

DEBORAH

THE TIME: 1973

SCENE 1

A hubcap-shaped Connecticut gymnasium.

LUCAN: I appreciate it even more—the mildness is terrific. Is your telephone still hooked-up downstairs?

THE DAUPHIN: You know it's not the same number as when you used to call all the time.

VIC PIANO: Why don't we just make this easy for both of us?

THE DAUPHIN: This is strictly business then.

LUCAN (nibbling at roast guinea fowl in a veloute sauce): Strictly business.

VIC PIANO: Is there a tape running?

THE DAUPHIN: Yeah.

LUCAN: You better catch it. I'm not the only one to believe that a deaf-mute girl read the lips of a Las Vegas entertainer planning to bomb a famous UFO museum. How do you like my striped suit? If you do anything to jeopardize this program, I'm going to get you!

VIC PIANO: You want this excitement . . . this . . . this action— just as much as I do!

THE DAUPHIN: No one lives to violate my wife and talk about it!

LUCAN: *I* live to violate your wife and talk about it!

VIC PIANO: It sounds like a woman.

THE DAUPHIN: How did you know that?

LUCAN: Instinct, I guess.

SCENE 2

A conference room.

LUCAN heats a pan of quartered tomatoes and sautés shrimp. The color change in the shrimp can be seen. When they are done, they curl up.

LUCAN: The chimes ring, the dogs bark. Cheese sandwiches in a panel truck. And oh...the violins! The lady says "May I have this dance?" I would be most delighted...

THE DAUPHIN: You're dreaming, Lucan. It's never going to be that simple again, that...that safe.

VIC PIANO (chewing a piece of truffled sausage encased in piecrust): But for you and me, Dauphin?

THE DAUPHIN: Can't you see? We're dying...we're dying in time to our own beautiful symphony of parting chariots.

   (They impulsively embrace and kiss.)

LUCAN: ...cherubs beneath an extinguished lamp.

THE DAUPHIN: I remember a baseball called a nickel rocket, men.

THE OTHERS: A baseball called a nickel rocket, sir!

VIC PIANO: How is Judy doing?

LUCAN: As a matter of fact, very well. She's even beginning to think a little like the old man.

THE DAUPHIN: What do you mean?

SCENE 3

A congressional hearing room.

LUCAN: . . . she said she wished she could have spent an evening with the jailhouse rocker.

THE DAUPHIN: The action would include some inspired pussy humping and crotch rubs that would burn your eyes out.

VIC PIANO: Right off the bat, people will say "there's good fucking and bad fucking." Why let them go on and on and on and on and on and on, their penises sliding into their vaginas. Fucking . . . there are so many ways of thinking about it. Here's the worst fucking list of doctors I ever saw: Dr. Bernard Schulman, Dr. Irvington Solomon, Dr. Theodore Martens, Dr. Craig Bushel, Dr. Sally Bloom, Dr. Richard L. Lumis, Dr. Peter Sibel, Dr. Theoharis Ariola. It's always, "Dispose of his body, Ginger, and for crisakes Let's Fuck!" They always want media attention.

THE DAUPHIN: You put the carrot before the cart—my father used to promise them a girl-packed UFO show.

VIC PIANO: These orchids I discovered nearly thirty years ago in certain forests of Burma. They occur at extremely rare intervals—traditionally only once in a century. From these orchids I have at last obtained, after twenty-five years of study, an essential oil which completes a particular formula—the formula elixir vitae for which the old philosophers sought in vain.

THE DAUPHIN: What a story! A beautiful stranger warns the 100 that she intends to track them down single-handed! What a scoop it would be to discover who she is!

VIC PIANO (pouring the men hefty glasses of local cognac, giving them steaming bowls of homemade soup, and heaping their plates with meat): You'd only be writing her obituary! She hasn't a chance against the 100! Those hoods have a finger in every racket in the area!

THE DAUPHIN: Simmer down! Johnny Adonis, the convicted

murderer scheduled to die in the electric chair tonight, wants you to see him in the death house, immediately!

VIC PIANO: Can't understand why!

THE DAUPHIN (covering the microphone with his hand): It's those little things that nag you.

VIC PIANO: They nettle at you.

SCENE 4

The setting is the same as Scene 2, though the sound of mopeds is not quite so thunderous.

(When Wu Ch'i owned a restaurant, there was a cook who, before dinner, was unable to control his ardour. He advanced and fried a pair of dumplings and returned. Wu Ch'i ordered him to be beheaded. The maitre d' admonished him, saying: "This is a talented cook; you should not behead him."
Wu Ch'i replied: "I am confident he is a cook of talent, but he is disobedient."
Thereupon he beheaded him.
The son of the son of this hapless cook was VERNON.)

It's about four o'clock in the afternoon. Shadows begin to worm their way across the stage. A $600 stallion belt buckle holds up VERNON's trousers.

LUCAN: I look older when I smoke. Don't let my age fool you.

THE DAUPHIN: How old are you?

LUCAN: I was launched in '51.

VERNON: You're jerkin' him off, toots.

THE DAUPHIN: No—how old are you?

LUCAN (heatedly): 22!!

SCENE 5

A hotel lobby.

DEBORAH sits across the couch from JUDY who is folding a section of newspaper. The couch is badly in need of reupholstering.

JUDY (reading from the paper): Octogenarians "Die" in Crash. Peter J. Reichwein, 82 years old, and his wife, Lois, 82 of Wayne, were "killed" yesterday when their car crashed into a slow-moving train at a crossing. Due, in large part, to the miraculous speed with which they were delivered into surgery, doctors were able to revive the New Jersey couple after two hours of confirmed forensic "death." Interest heightened amid reports from attendant hospital personnel that a voluble and robust Reichwein later recalled the experience of participating in this exchange at the instant of "expiration": "What do you mean bringing a platinum cutie into a respectable establishment like this?" "Platinum cutie!!! Men, surround this oaf! Make it so champagne bubbles will never tickle his nose again!! Fix him so another wax dame will never make him balmy!" "You will do no such thing, Captain!" "Draw your weapon from its scabbard!" "You are about to become extinct, Captain! Never again to strengthen alliances or encourage troops to succor the poor!" "You're a shit, sir . . . a real shit!!" "I'm going to cleave your brains in two—I hope they don't regenerate like worm-parts, Captain!!" "It is you sir, who will soon adorn my hook !!!" "Your fish-like countenance strikes me as familiar, Captain—have we sparred before?" "You too ring a visual bell, sir, but I too cannot locate the source." "Let us agree then that the survivor of this skirmish trace the wellspring of this faint familiarity." "If it is I, sir, I will employ in my investigation every possible means —electronic bloodpressure units, calculators that are as thin as credit cards, wrist microsplit stopwatches." "Taste death, then, Captain!" "Taste death then to you sir."

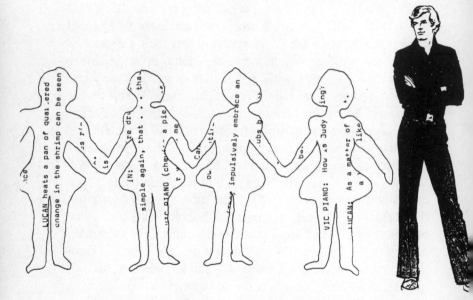

Sun Tzu Drilling the Concubines of King Ho-lu

I SMELL
ESTHER WILLIAMS

for Rachel "Calamity" Jane Horowitz

Shivering Beneath The Blue Clouds
Having An Aperitif With A
Name From The White Pages

Reading about nitrogen fixation, that process that lays the
foundation for the synthesis of proteins, the sadness of my
friends popped into my mind and I admitted the possibility that
I had read instead of the authoritative text, Speer's memoirs
entitled *Inside The Third Reich*.

Here's to the syphilitic world and its sullen lugubrious days
and the recrudescence of family turmoil in pockets across an
individual's map—and I am not the individual and things
cease being what they are not, and I stop
this
here,   and sip

To ask, once out of the bar mitzvah brunch, is our convivial
relative waiting, like Vitamin A in the retina, to be discovered

or is he making profit out of sacred things or is he too much the
naif for simony; or to accept someone who says, I saw him
before picking his nose at a red light—and to ask, who is this
splenetic image deflator. These treaties exist in name only.
And, under the circumstances, they doubt him "stalwart"
enough to resist the temptation to flee, but only one burro has
the energy to bray for him.

How bummed, to be fuelless in these futuristic boondocks
with this synesthesia of some before and the taste of this
medium point like a dentist's finger in my mouth.

I drew my shades a crack (life's been good to me so far)
(Everyone thinks orange juice is good and cigarettes are bad—
but I like both of them) and poured a glass of orange juice and
looked for a cigarette ("If only I could find one!"). I don't
remember anything after that. Let's see, I opened the shades a
tiny bit...I got some juice...or maybe made some and then
had it, I couldn't find my pack of cigarettes...nope, I can't
remember a thing after that.

Isn't so and so a snob? She won't even admit she liked *Grease*.
I'd like to empty out her tube of Ortho cream and fill it with
Oscar's guacamole dip.

When I was looking at the quart container of milk I'd gotten
that morning, it reminded me of when I was a boy because it's
so little and skinny compared to the half-gallon we usually
buy. It led me to think about glandular disorders and growth
dysfunction—I was perusing the label on the bottle of Topco
Multiple vitamins. Topco Associates, Inc. is based in Skokie,
Illinois which, of course, had gained recent notoriety for the
Nazi-Jewish controversy. I looked at the clock and bolted. I

quote what's-her-name verbatim on the issue of promptness—
If you don't pick me up at 5:30 on the button, I'll beat you and
beat you until even your colleagues at the university won't
recognize you. This shows how inhuman she is because everyone knows how ignominious it is not to be recognized by one's
colleagues.

I was talking to Napoleon's sister—she's living with these
African natives; the kinds that have saucers in their lips and
their hair shaped at the top into Milkbones. They carried her on
a vine litter to her house. She had a comparatively nice place.

"He wouldn't have liked what they did with him," she was
saying, "he was so into the earth—y'know—he'd wanna be
with it."

She turned her attention to a cheese cart that her son was
inching towards.

"Didn't you just play with the dog?"

He nodded.

"Well wash your hands . . . c'mon now."

TEENAGE CHRIST KILLERS

Mother: Where were you?

Moshe ⎱
Chaim ⎰ Out.

Mother: Where!?

Moshe ⎱
Chaim ⎰ Just out.

It's Wednesday in Tokyo. Here it's Tuesday. In Denver it's
Monday. On Saturn, it's Christmas for the 93rd consecutive
day this week. We should begin to think of jogging, beyond
the therapeutic and recreational. NASA knows this and is

developing a sneaker. Bio-feedback will be used to teach runners to produce, within the body, a glandular form of Tang. A camphorated tincture of colorless remarks like "it's murder, but I love it" and "it's the only body I've got" will be used to tranquilize hostile aliens. You'll hear more about this, as we do, darling. For now, my arms are nude. A breeze from the window at the foot of the bed excites the hairs.

MOVIE SCRIPT

Two plastic containers of shampoo sitting at the edge of a tub —I don't know, one might be Revlon or Breck, the other, a little fancier, maybe Vidal Sassoon or something: one says to the other "I like your back-to-school sweater," the other says, "I never get to watch sports on t.v. anymore." The phone rings—I'm on the can—for the 53rd day, trying to break Dimaggio's other record. A guy on the radio says that the concrete shortage is over—I get the hell off the john, saying "fuck this." I go get some concrete shoes made and form a rock band called "Mafia Victims." We volunteer to tour oil-rich nations as "musical ambassadors" in the tradition of Louis Armstrong. Things don't pan out quickly enough—I get itchy. I try to form a Sonny and Cher type act with a really talented ticketing agent from Frontier Airlines. We flounder around for a while and she eventually takes an accounting job in Atlanta. I volunteer to become the world's first human study lamp. I'm sold to a sophomore pre-law student at Harvard. He turns out to be Edward Kennedy. The rest of the movie can be about Joe and JFK and Bobby, and Ted's back problems, his senatorial career, Chappaquiddick, his wife Joan's battle with alcoholism, etc.

July 2: I have the Pathet Lao dream again. Insurgents, some fidgeting with the drawstrings that hold their pajama bottoms up, expropriate all the apartment's furniture. I establish psychic communication with the couch and extrapolate, from bits and pieces of information, the whereabouts of the rebels' sanctuary. I make reservations with an airline. I pack and rush to the terminal. I walk back and forth, from one end to the other—apparently the airline doesn't exist.

The bone of contention lodged in the throats of Wall Street pundit, armchair investor, and consumer alike was simply this: would the new, lighter, less caloric beer sell or did the putative American penchant for vigor and lankness pale in the face of pretzel sticks and a foamy head? Light beer advocates could obviously point to the success of its sister industry's parallel "line"—the low tar cigarette. But was obesity the compelling concern that cancer of the lungs or throat had turned out to be? I think that for one brief moment, no one knew!

My head felt like an aluminum pod filled with loose Klaxon peas. I felt like running to someone and hiding it between her breasts. . . . That morning I'd seen the doctors—they'd looked into my ear and seen the perforated drum, the spot of blood, the protective clog of wax, the trapped pool of water. Veteran explorers of ancient rocks believe that cell nuclei may have originated 1.4 billion years ago—not 600 million, as is widely supposed. There is also Paul Jennings' observation: "When numbered pieces of toast and marmalade were dropped on various samples of carpet arranged in quality from coir matting to the finest Kirman rugs, the marmalade-downwards incidence (Mdi) varied indirectly with the quality of the carpet (Qc)—the Principle of the Graduated Hostility of Things."

Certain sectors of the citizenry, such as the housewife, must not be neglected. They must be enabled to matriculate and take courses like Introduction to Is Johnny Mathis Really Black? and Advanced How Come Sophia Loren Has Made Nine Pictures With Marcello Mastroianni If She Is So In Love With Her Husband, Carlo Ponti. They must be prepared to take the standardized Clank Shtup Exam.

Husbands must not act like moronic fans who jeer when their wives are losing and cheer when they win. Nor like hypercritical shades from the underworld.

That night I dreamt of the mullican—a huge crinite dugong-like sea mammal, thought to resemble, when beached and basking, those recumbent nudes of fin de siècle portraiture.

Dear Gregg: The waitress *has* got psychic powers. She put me in touch with my dead mother at lunch. . . . I don't want to talk about it. I nurture many dreams, but paramount is the hope that, someday, our camps have another skating party.

Mother called with her versions of Mickey Rooney's galvanizing exhortations from *Babes in Arms*. Though, without the advantages of phone-a-vision, I was helpless to determine if she had gone as far as to affect Rooney's two-story brilliantined pompadour.

Susan and Jill were so excited! They'd primped for weeks and the day had finally come! Is there anything more beautiful than a pair of girls consumed by romance! Jill stood in front of the mirror! Her underpants were a "yellow-pages" print! "Howard will flip!" Susan assured Jill! Susan was not to be outdone! She wore a diaphanous blouse! She was well-endowed and knew it! So did Jill! They were some luscious pair!

Across the street, Howard and Steve nervously gulped beer! Howard looked as if he'd stepped out of a training film! Steve seemed dissipated though! His hollow eye sockets distilled a purulent fluid! What turpitude had precipitated this dissolution?! What did Susan see in him?! Jill tended her own beeswax in this matter!

Jill couldn't eat a thing! Susan fried eggs and sausage! The smell pervaded the small house! "What a silly stench!" Jill giggled! "I get hungry when I'm excited...and I'm starving!" Susan blushed! Jill sniffed at her armpits and shook her head, "You can't smell anything in this room!" "Speaking of smells," Susan said, "I hope their parts are pleasant!"

"Are you sure you don't mind having Clare for the week?"

"No, no."

"Because I could always get a professional baby-sitter...it would be a strange woman...but..."

"No no no, I'd love to have Clare. Where are you two going anyway?"

"Brussels."

"Do you know where to stay?"

"Arthur Frommer recommends The Hotel Cecil, 13 Blvd. du Jardin Botanique corner of the Blvd. Adolphe Max directly on the Place Rogier."

"That sounds like a nice place."

"You sure you don't mind staying with Clare? We could get a woman from an agency—she might turn out to be a mutilator or junkie or something—one of those women who puts the kid in the oven and tucks the turkey in...but if it's less trouble..."

"No no no...it's no bother."

A gentlemen from the apartment complex is stockpiling torpedoes, X-ray specs, switchblade combs, flesh eating plants, exploding pens, black soap and sneezing powder. All morning he knocks boiled eggs into the garbage disposal with a facsimile of the tamping iron that shot through the head of Phineas P. Gage at Cavendish, Vermont, Sept. 14, 1848.

"Shouldn't he be working?"

He should be, but someone at Oil of Olay Summer Camp taught him to maintain a constant vigilance. When he puts his records on, he thinks of her sucking his cock. He paints a phone booth on the wall and goes in it and calls her. Then he bugs her all afternoon. Eventually they marry. He finds work in the field of "auto salvage." She bears a daughter. At twelve, the daughter's body blossoms. She spends her afternoons smoking cigarettes and listening to records with her friends, exchanging a regicidal wink now and then with a girl who plays with her hair—the clouds becoming darker and darker blue—one girl repeats something she'd heard from an older friend about love-making being like watching a World War II movie with Red Buttons.

The clandestine organization (The Hardware Moguls) that was playing her for a chump taped her boyfriend's conversation: "Oon WHIS-key kon SO-dah, por fah-VOR" ("Please mix me a drink of whiskey and soda") and "PAH-rah me SO-loh, kon AH-wah natu-RAHL" ("I shall take mine straight, with plain water"). When they interrogated him in the A&P parking lot, he broke down:

"What in god's name do you want from me—I told you—I have no...no journal—I'm a...bank clerk...an ordinary garden variety bank clerk."

"Oh yeah? What's an Individual Retirement Account?"

"An Individual Retirement Account is a personal tax-sheltered retirement plan. It was developed by Congress to bring to every American worker the opportunity to build a more secure future for himself and for his family."

"Who can establish an account?"

"Retirement accounts are available to any wage-earner."

"Can my spouse establish one?"

"Your working spouse may establish a separate account

too, provided she is not currently a participant in an employer-sponsored plan.''

''Do I pay taxes on the income earned by my account?''

Phil! Phil! Phil! Phil! Phil! Phil! Phil wasn't Typhoid Mary's son and we never, *never* had a duel with shish kebab skewers over the same girl, but he did work his way through two years of UCLA as a make-up man's assistant with the Mack Sennett crew, though something about that droopy-lidded, wheels-turning-in-the-head gaze of his reminds one of Brad Darrach's description of Bobby Fischer, ''Alone, uncounseled, jouncing to rock music in a borscht-belt hotel, Bobby had outgeneraled the mighty Soviet chess establishment.'' Phil! Phil! Phil! Here's Phil—holding a dish towel and pan as he listens to ''Refillable Dispenser Raga'' coming from the radio in a neighbor's car... when suddenly Phil yells in the direction of a body hidden under the hood of the idling Chevy Nova, ''Hey! ...etc. . . . .'' To try to alleviate nervous tension and insomnia, Phil submits himself to the Kneip treatment—a form of hydrotherapy that requires him to take cold baths.

A man and woman (who looks like Katherine Ross) sink down into the hot foliage in a film version of Harold Robbins' *The Adventurers*.

The stag party goes on until breakfast and she's beginning to feel hungry again. Well, the organist is high and he's playing ''Needles and Pins''. The bride's name is Sirloin Stockade. Her real name is Bonnie from Phase I.

If a muscular Italian is pushing you higher and higher on a swing and you fall—high in an arc to the hard packed sand— the nuns will take care of you and you will have my baby. Don't cry.

THE MONSTER

The Monster hates you because you melted her Conway Twitty 45s. But here we are again! You in your cardigan sweater with the letter you won in gymnastics. Hickory smoke from the barbeque curling towards the perfume of the bath. The Hatfields and McCoys downstairs at their annual conclave. The village chiropractor pedaling up our front path, the litter of dachshunds asleep in their box under the striped tent. But doesn't it bother you that you weren't enough of a fusspot to see that the lawn service people raked near the patio and got rid of those detestably allergenic puffballs?

It was a time of uncertain leisure, a time of faulty parachutes, of an uncertain public's mandate for pyrotechnic child care, of the two-handed backhand with tons of topspin. And over the years the sun cooled as if it were a tablespoon of bisque that Yahweh was blowing on.

A macadam path lined with quackgrass and pokeweeds stretched down the hill towards P.S. 231 Harry Moore School and in the shadow of Togo Mountain, beneath a pastel sky, Amos the Weimaraner puppy, played by Jackie Cooper, felt like Pascal among his variety of books. Then the Monster came and offered him vichyssoise from a swollen can, but Amos balked and, dropping his bundles of text into a pasteboard portmanteau, loped...towards the Newark drive-in movie showing *Kung Fu Zombies Drink Campari*. And later, when the delivery man came to install the pad and shag carpet, the Monster (unable to get a job because of her weight) cozened the workmen, with untapped girlishness, into converting her storm windows to tinted insulating glass.

AUGUST

The pig's out of the pen. Grandma can't speak. My heart is
about to explode. Negative-three: see how you look—crooked
blouse minus a button, disheveled trousers, zipper jammed
halfway. Negative-two: "maybe we'll have a meatless-friday
with your baited ponytail." Negative-one: they've been
watching *your* programs all night. Zero: whose idea was it to
stock the pool with carp for the labor day potlatch. First of all,
I don't believe in the star system or nepotism and I've seen
political patronage first-hand, having lived in Jersey City. Second of all, a potato-dumpling-riding show is a crystal meth
image and not something to mention while I'm calling home.
Third of all, when you're done throwing flour at those chops,
think about going to the store for air freshener. Deodorant for
this chapel. "We smell from the speed. And we're about to
jump into a bracing pool of matrimony, of tax relief, of surfing
and snoring...marry me you piece, you unwitting pawn in a
brand...new...negligee!" I like that big pink cyst on his
fishing pole. August...drum corps season, you can see the
veterinarian's office I designed, from this B-52 of an apartment.

Rakish crescent moon, does thin hair require combing or
brushing? You want to comb my hair? You want me to remove
my hat which I bought in Maine—so you can see my hair and
sort of diagnose its needs? It's difficult to hear—someone's
playing that whale album again.

The very tender message is not drawn above a resort beach by
propeller plane, but left, say, between the cup and saucer of
one's fancy. The element of suspense attending such a message's reply is said to be what goaded Bob into just forgetting it
and he celebrated the easing of his burden in a park adjacent to

the bait store. Drugs...sure, Bob took a few. Cheated the government? No more than the rest of us. Swallowed his gum every once in a while. Puts his pants on one leg at a time. Socks. Shoes. Buttons his shirt. Knots and adjusts his necktie. Winds his watch. Slips his jacket on. Quick cup of coffee. Puts water in the dog's bowl. The car-pool honks. Out he goes. Not the most nutritious breakfast in the world—but so it goes. Day after day. With the thump of each new headline upon the front porches of our people—the North-Americans.

Digging for family roots, one may unearth an uncle who delighted in sniffing professional women's tennis players' "dew-laden" socks, (which, left to the winter night, provide an image of "frost encrusted socks"). National security, though, like the discovery of penicillin, may be served by providential accident. Video espionage mistakenly applied, for example, to room 325 instead of 225, may reveal an unemployable emigré, an idiot-savant with a funny accent in a long smock with a rattan cane, (one imagines him waving goodbye to the inflation-ravaged Western European nations whose citizens have been forced to choose between college for their children and air-conditioning for their homes), designing a bomb that would, regardless of the site of detonation, seek out and shatter Alexander Haig. But Secret Service agent and mermaid alike—my caveat for either would be identical: a summer cold can be pretty terrible if you don't take care of it. Good health doesn't have to be an accident.

I'LL BE WEARING GOLDEN ARCHES

I.

I think I'm wearing largemouth bass instead of sneakers, this afternoon. I think they're laced through the eyes. I had better butter my magazine and put a band-aid on my watch band, your honor. Yak. Yak. Yak. And eat the article and nurse the time. I'd better cool the braggadocio and savor the silt and retire my Kodak to its pouch case. Vat's dis katzenjammer? (She can't stand his bruxistic slumber...) Your honor, this is a kangaroo court... A Central-Asiatic couldn't get a fair hearing within 10,000 miles of this room. It behooves ya to eeeck out a living before they usurp your jurisdiction. Before I pour a quart of koumiss on this tinsel town. It's late, shut the gate. Listen for the katydid.

II.

The Inquisitor: What will you be wearing?

Me: Just... peds.

The Inquisitor: I can't hear you.

Me: Just peds!

The Inquisitor: 50 more lashes!

Me: Arrrrgh! No! No!

The Inquisitor: What'll you be wearing then?!

Me: Wedgies.

The Inquisitor: Prepare the thumb-screws!

Me: Pumps!

The Inquisitor: Ready the rack!

Mc: Wing-tipped Oxfords!

III.

Dawn breaks over the cabin and lake. The Rat Pack —Sinatra, Martin, Lawford, Davis—is drinking booze and horsing around with the bread dough bait that their guide has prepared.

IV.

As time robs moisture from our skin, death beckons. We sing: "It's a hell of a way to go / noshing on herring and nagging each other / but we're just hired stooges / getting laid off by death."

V.

This is my feeling: Should the citizens, who people the slopes which descend from the abscissa, be segregated according to blood-sugar levels —those designated "X" doomed to an eternity of vending mother-of-pearl plaques and gold baubles at roadside stands —those dubbed "Y" left to rattle the bars of their proscenium calaboose? Wheat must be sold. Tradeswoman, meatman, fishmonger, and furrier must thrive. Commerce must hum as time traipses by.

Additionally, there is life's diverting aspect, e.g. making a toast in one of many languages, "hunting" a lightning bug, tickling someone who's drinking at a fountain, even ballooning or carving and painting miniature wooden animals. Finally, there is a wetter aspect, which includes singing in the shower or participating in a swim meet.

The Autocron's girlfriend slipped out of her peignoir and tossed it across his miniature schnauzer which he adored more than his hordes of minions. When he went outside to get the paper, he noticed that the dew had become frost and, noting that the frost was architecturally complex although it could not literally house anyone, reasoned that a bubble's tenant was simply air. His adjutant walked up the front path and said "Good morning, you have to drive your sister somewhere today." The Autocron said, "Where? I thought I had today to myself." The adjutant's breath smelled mediciney and he said, "She needs a ride to the Lodge Hall where she'll be singing tonight . . . she needs to rehearse." After breakfast, when the Autocron got into his car, he noticed scores of sand nicks in his windshield. He wondered whether he should ask his father for the money for a new windshield. He wondered whether insurance would cover the replacement. He wondered whether bearing the cost himself wouldn't prevent him from being able to afford the rent if his girlfriend got the H.E.W. job in Washington and moved out.

"Rouse the stevedores from their atmospheric bistro — we sail at dawn!" I said. While I was heating up some beans, later, I decided to have a braunschweiger sandwich with a yogurt dressing. (I'd just gotten back from visiting my parents in New Jersey.) I was reading Rex Morgan M.D. in the Post — Morgan's standing behind some woman who's on the phone — she's saying, Vince please — listen to me — CLICK — Morgan looks up at her looking at the phone and says, Did he hang up on you, Connie? And she says, We — We must have been cut off. I'm one of those purists who can't ignore a blurry television picture and still enjoy the show. If the networks were taking a survey and asking which programs I preferred, though, I'd be hard put to say. What could I do with the survey-taker? I don't know morse-code, or the language of the deaf or Esperanto for "If I do not come out soon, keep going around the block" or "I love girls who smell like chewing gum. . . . like the ones at the all-night dermatologist's office." Three years ago in Hempstead, N.Y. where I was doing research in low-temperature physics, I had an experience with survey-takers. A couple appeared at my door one evening, with sheafs of questions. The second I let them in, the gentleman flew to the metallic globe I kept on my coffee table. The young lady was sweet and self-effacing and beguiling. But it was ridiculously beautiful the way he brandished the globe above his head as if to whack himself with a how-would-you-like-a-punch-in-the-nose attitude — his cerebral hemispheres parting like red seas, like masses yearning to be free, revealing down the center of his head, a black-top shuffleboard court with miniature retired people on it.

"A lot of aches and pains go with the territory," Craig assured a pair of junior partners cornered against a cupboard in the butler's pantry. And Kay teetered by, hailing Craig's attention y'know —shaking hands with herself, the way she does, and went, "Craig Newcomer, if you'd put that drink down for one little second and come over here and . . ." Now Craig's coming over and Kay goes "Look, I'm sittin here and I think I'm payin real good attention and all of a sudden I turn my back—it's autumn. Y'know —wha'did it do, creep up on me or what? Get coy? What?" Craig takes her by the shoulders and points her towards the veranda, "What do you want the seasons to do, Kay," he says, "hit you on the head when they change?" And, oh my, there's Beatrice and her driving instructor friend dressed to commit homicide. But soon, fear of Yankee patrols makes further conversation taboo. Bang. As sweating rack boys push carts loaded with suits, coats and dresses, a Schlitz sales representative in a goat costume is convulsed by a neuromuscular spasm after being shot by a burp gun.

Rachel left on Friday. . . I'm saying this because I want everyone to know how sad I am.
You think that's bad?
What do you mean?
I know someone who was swimming in his pool and drowned —*that's* sad.
Who was he?
That Rolling Stone —Brian Jones.
You really knew him?
Naaa . . . I just read about him, really.

I don't know what to say.
How about "I'm very sorry."
I am . . . very very sorry. I know he played a seminal role in the formation of the group.

(The water-skiers gave us a shower as they passed. Then we were deloused and had to go to prison.)

MOVIE SCRIPT

George Washington Carver stands in an Alabama field scratching his head, fanning a thin, sensitive visage with his cap. A rain-washed gully, (of the sort that scourges Southern farm land starved for inorganic mineral salts—desperate for the cyclic replenishment of crop rotation), is *always* an annoying place to break a plow handle, but poor Professor Carver's troubles are just beginning. "Oh, no!" he says, "Here comes a bunch of Tuskegee coeds!" He knows they'll be mean, meaner than any of the girls he'd ever dated. He looks around for a place to hide, but before he thinks to climb in the wagon and cover himself with seed bags, they're on him. These girls have foraged enough leaf mold to be expert botanists, but the only instruments they plan to use on Carver's stalk are their mouths and slits. For women who lead lives like this, it's nothing to take an unwilling guy and put him through their paces. In fact, a gang bang is like normal sex for these creeps. But for Carver, it's a whole new trip. At first, it was one he'd wished he missed. He'd never even been to bed with two girls, let alone make it in public. But there's little discourse in situations like this, and no choices either. Once they've spotted his firm slender ass, there's no way they'll leave without seeing — and feeling and fucking—a lot more. As each item of clothing is torn away, he feels his demure personality as a research professor at Tuskegee Institute also disappearing—along with his former sexual inhibitions. Since the greedy coeds don't bother to take turns with him, but rather have him all at once, the action makes his head spin—or is it the rough hands and soggy, steaming cunts that make him dizzy? After this, going back to the old way would seem anticlimactic. But later that evening, Carver is attacked by Blacula.

These are very dear to me—these notes—very expensive and uncertain and childish. I'm writing them every day. Tonight I feel very lonely—Rachel's gone to Bermuda with her family and the apartment is empty. I'm a little apprehensive about my visit with Barbara in Lansing—but more hopeful than apprehensive, really. I'm looking forward to human contact that's un-habitual and un-mapped—my latest estimate is that certain forms of human relations are redemptive. I probably still have firm expectations in mind vis-a-vis un-mapped human contact and vis-a-vis Barbara in Lansing and vis-a-vis these notes—what a typically topical malady. This will be tonight's final entry then:

Bob was saying, I'll never bring Sharon over again—I'm so sorry. . . About what, I said. About her knocking the idol off your speaker cabinet. C'mon, I said, that's nothing—that's ridiculous. What bothered me was her breaking that glass. Those glasses were the first things I bought for the apartment. I got the pieces of the broken glass which I kept wrapped in a few pages of the Denver Post. As I was showing them to Bob, he suddenly turned white. What? I asked. I swear to god, he said, I swear to god I saw them move! He spoke very little the rest of the evening and hasn't broached the subject since.

Because nothing is so overtaxed as the network of cybernetic checks and balances that averts and thwarts rash judgment, system fatigue is an inevitable fact of life whether it literally advertises itself as in the case of those improvident, precipitantly released Hollywood pageants ("am I nuts or what?") that, in the phraseology of the trade magazines "snooze into the market;" or whether it hides its head under the covers of police paperwork, hearsay, and miscellaneous clue, as in the instance of the FBI-wired county official with severe tachycardiac spasms who chose mistakenly between instant gratification and a fifteen minute ride to medication; or whether it surfaces in a cherub-cheeked appliance heiress unwittingly surrendering her heart and purse strings to a philandering chiseler, whose unctuous good looks are matched only by his unprincipled greed, in the shadows which caress the kiosk's colonnettes like a gossamer bunting during this lush Virginia fall twilight.

I unbuttoned my jacket, loosened my tie, scratched a mosquito bite on her calf and rose to brush my tongue before kissing beautiful Maria Ragazza, Carlo Gambino's ex-wife. As I spit hurriedly into the sink, I turned to see her clawing a red pit in her calf where the bite had been. You did this to me, she hissed. I rushed to her side and buried my kisses into the raw gouge. When the skin heals, I said, my kisses will be interred in your calf! Her face trembled like a leaf on an antenna. We kissed. I apprehended the kiss modally. The Labial Protasis: initially, the predominant sensation is of full slick tumid quivering catholic lips / Le Temps de la Langue: the tongue sweeps the lips with excruciating luxury and delves assertively into the mouth, playfully jousting its counterpart—its "jumeau d'amour" / The Orifice Complexus (also Swinburne Phase and rarely Tartar's Play): simply—the active hungering mouth in febrile animalistic dilation and systole.

The bassoon seems to say, what do you know about setting up a business letter? and the strings seemingly retort in unison, as much as you do! Who was it that couldn't find the key to the xerox machine after being here six months. An impish staccato passage from the first violins recalls the Czech "Furiant", a lively Bohemian dance in 3/4 meter, and, with its sudden changes from melancholy to exuberance, evokes Dvorak's "Dumky Trio." As the timpani and basses augur an almost subterranean ritardando, the orchestra segues into a bucolic

conciliatory movement that seems to suggest, this office is like
an eco-system—managerial duties, secretarial duties, main-
tenance responsibilities, switchboard and messenger service
—all mesh in a synergetic, mutually advantageous hierarchy,
that necessarily precludes petty squabbles and bitching.

MERCERNARIES UNEARTH JOMO KENYATTA'S "PRIVATE STASH"

The rugged family room atmosphere would have been shat-
tered had the Guffs known that the poodles were suffocating in
their station wagon. But soon they would find the still poodles.
Let's eavesdrop:

> Pop: Dogs don't grow on trees, son.
>
> Little Roy: Why Pop? You said they put Con-
> fucius and Candy in the ground—just like we
> did when we planted seeds for Greta's garden.
>
> Pop: Son, what do you say we both get some
> hunks of knockwurst and catch that Denver
> Bronco game we've been waiting for?
>
> Little Roy: Super idea, Pop!!!!
>
> Pop: Super *Bowl,* son!

Re: Lansing visit with Barbara. I, Mark Leyner, repudiate
everything I said about uncharted human relations. The first
night in Lansing, we fucked three times—each time more
tedious than the one before. She kept wanting more more more
more more satisfaction. For four days she talked about her heat
without let-up, like a disgusting pig . . . always with a bottle of
Tab jammed into her mouth—a shiny red mouth that seemed
like the only sign of life enshrouded in the dough of her fat
flesh. Uh-oh Barbara's coming—I better stop and put this
away.

Every person at the colloquium thought Kathleen an over-weening prima donna. And when round robin discussion opened, more depressing invective than ever filled the shape of its container. In a parade, they unfurled their skeins of initials. With craven unanimity, they blasted Kathleen with their ill-conceived and pleonastic implosions. But still, amidst this wilting, Kathleen (a little drunk) delivered her statements inviting the very adversaries present before her to give up, to lie down, to die, to rot, to become ant food.

Today, people look for ''fiber'' in their food like Ponce de Léon looking for the fountain of youth—the pool of puerility that's been cussed and discussed. That's as real as a pome-granate poo-bah. But her rear looks like a cleft pomegranate, but her rear is a red herring. The real issue is her royal flush of boyfriends that runs from Jerk to Asshole.

The aroma of green tinder imbued his albums and bloodmobile & when he saw wisps of her by the rigid percolator, his eyes rolled like egg yolks on a piano bench being moved from room to room, and his hand was observed by witnesses in a town five miles away, around the neck of a bottle of Chivas Regal.

They kissed, but the warm contents of her mouth troubled him like an automat's pot-luck. And the Tudor arches afforded an incomplete view of her bus.

The affidavit states that he said ''Ahoy there!'' when he arrived. That she chewed and swallowed a photograph of his swami. He lists ''choking on a piece of food at an embassy party'' as his #1 phobia; she lists ''the smell of gasoline'' as her favorite olfactory turn-on, and ''giving myself paper-cuts'' as her most debilitating hobby.

"What a beautiful gun...more beautiful than the three pointed at your back, amigo."

"Give it to me straight. I can take it. How long do I have?" "About two seconds." "Put that gun down!" "After all the misery you've put me through..." "Misery? What misery?!"

I made a mental catalogue of the spread: a rosewood desk on embossed "lion's paw" legs / photograph of a woman in filoplume hat and child on a mechanical hobby-horse / golfball paperweight / an overturned rosewood windsor chair / a disarray of legal and steno pads and pencils / a half-torn letter reading "... ght. Can't we begin again —without suspicions and recriminations —can't we say to each other —I made a mistake —that each night I spent apart from you was filled with sadness and emptiness —because that's how it was for me. If only you hadn't..." / a bust of Nefertiti / a calendar-penholder / a set of windows with drawn shades / a coatrack / an oriental-style taboret / a Morris chair with dark green chamois leather cushions / an open bottle of gin on a mock-filigree fold-out bar / an ashtray filled with butts, some bearing lipstick traces.

She coughed—a dainty little cough like that of an antique miniature Basin-Pull steam engine.
"Shoot" I said.
She opened her pocketbook and took out a plaid cloth-covered cigarette box. In a slow, cautious, unassumingly economical motion, I reached into my vest pocket and withdrew a lighter which I displayed in the air before flicking. She leaned over and, smoothing a wisp of hair behind her ear, lit her cigarette. She took a quick nervous puff and fidgeted with a loose thread at the hem of her skirt and then with the chipped plastic viridine green button over one of the mock pockets of her blouse.

"Shoot" I said.

She gnawed at a hang-nail briefly and then tugged at the charm bracelet at her wrist. Crossing and uncrossing her legs, she scratched a discolored patch of flesh on her cheek. She kicked one of her pumps off, slid it under the chair with her foot, and loosened the nainsook Montpellier green bow at her collar.

"Shoot" I said.

I've got to get some rest now —tomorrow's leather pounding time —flat-footing . . . gumshoeing . . . hawkshawing . . .
what's in a name anyway —tomorrow the sun rises —I shake the bones out of my hair —rinse the sea-weed out of my mouth —palliate these gripping cramps with some luke-warm juice and go out and make a dirty god damn shit-eating motherfucking buck. My name's Leyner . . . Mark Leyner —I wasn't born with that name —I earned it . . . believe me.

THE ROSEATE SPOONBILL
(Comments after the death of
John D. Rockefeller 3d)

It's difficult to empathize with anyone. But it's like impossible to comprehend the fright with which one, after not having been home for literally years —the fright with which one reaches into his old bureau —into his tenebrous grotto of a drawer —the fright with which one reaches into a drawer, right, and into the unsympathetic length of his tattiest dowdiest widowed sock and have like pains shoot up his dorsal environs. You want to say "see you in the funny papers" and burrow straight under that Disneyesque counterpane immediately. Life is, au fond, not for the chicken-hearted. Stan Musial, when he was physical fitness consultant to the president in '65 wrote, " . . . there is no equality of opportunity —in education, in employment, or in any other area —for persons who are weak and lethargic, timid and awkward, or lacking in energy and the basic physical skills.''

What considerations must be taken into account when looking for a man to marry? Can, for instance, one woman's priorities accommodate both astrological affinity *and* the extent to which a gentleman has built up equity? And what form does that equity take? Has it been accumulated in a piecemeal, haphazard manner, consisting of, say, a television, stereo, toaster, wardrobe, clock-radio, and turquoise ring or two? Is its value apparent only with respect to a certain connoisseur-ship, as in the case of my friend Randall Schroth's antique car?

In this regard, what occupies the mind of someone like Brooke Shields' mother? Miss Shields, whose pool of nuptial possibil-ity is rife with the most conniving piranha. Has the thought of an arranged marriage not occurred to the mother of this extraordinary girl? An arranged marriage of the sort that was common in a host of venerable cultures, including the Akwe-Shavante Indians of Central Brazil and the Heian court of 10th century Japan.

Although judging from coeval texts such as *The Pillow-Book of Sei Shonagon* and *The Tale of Genji,* the feudal Japanese court boasted enough heavy action, (conducted surreptitiously behind screens of wattled bamboo or rather ostentatiously, in keeping with the fabulously amoral zeitgeist of the period), to curl hair upon the nape of the most coy and prim of hand-maidens' necks or to unravel the top-knot of even the most phlegmatic warrior.

Oh great, Werner from my soap opera "To Knot the Grey Nuts" is dying. That phony... It's good to see his hopes blow up in his face!

Ray thought it was funny that my toilet is coin-operated —but what does he think this apartment complex is, a public school? Up in the rarefied air of *my* income bracket, you get what you pay for, Ray!

The last thing she said was, "I'm about to be discovered. I've been pitting all my friends against each other."

So I said, "That's an intensely delicate operation to have undertaken. And I really admire intense individuals. In fact, people have said that I have a certain intensity. A certain 'I don't know what exactly.' A certain hunger for truth... a certain thirst for adrenaline maybe. Perhaps an unnatural affection for danger, a latent death wish... a kind of hopelessly self-destructive weltschmerz. Aren't you going to say anything?"

"I'm about to be discovered. I've been pitting all my friends against each other."

The October weather has been delightful. Like that crisp breeze just now. Did you see how rosy it made my cheeks? The playoff games have been more than body and soul can bear. Vitamin E has transformed my scalp into a fertile promised land. But the dead Pope looks like an ornate canary laid out that way.

Some afternoons, the sun hits my phonebook at just the right angle and light shimmers off its cover like shards of topaz. Other men may be stalled in traffic, asleep with their succubi. Other men may be sitting down to dinner already. These men eat too early! But we men are such a club. With our habits and clothes. We love to kiss babies when we campaign. And we love to drink coffee. And that accounts for the sheer voluminosity of our philosophies, all that coffee.

Ah, October whatever it is. I'm back in the saddle again. I'm the story of lovely lady who was very very very bewitching. As George Eliot said of Dorothea Brooke in *Middlemarch,* "Most men thought her bewitching when she was on horseback." I feel as if a sixteen ounce glove has softened the fist of fate's devastating uppercut. I feel as if horse tranquilizer has slowed the team that aproaches with my hearse. As if firemen have discovered new ladders, to discover me. The addlepated officer, retrieved, fighting a war that ended thirty-three years ago. The last of the Mohicans. The final Brontosaurus-burger sold on a Sat. night. Half swan, half doe. With feathers of Chantilly lace and hooves of translucent quartz.

On the other hand, I'm an insular queen amidst all this exalted glee, amidst these Visa cards and platters of cheese and smoked lox. Even when I'm playing bridge, I have to worry about my ex-husband's friends bombing my oil fields. In the dead of night, having to throw on a few things and go join the bucket line. It may be just a false alarm that a kid's idle hands turned in or a ruse contrived by my sister to get me to my surprise party! I don't know what to say. "For me?" or "You shouldn't have!" or simply "I don't know what to say." But the simultaneous sensation of rampant happiness and anxiety results in a kind of torsion that is exhilarating.
Aaaaaaahhh! To sleep, though, I need to be tapped not so gently on the forehead with a rubber mallet. Zzzzzzzzzzzzz . . .

It feels magnificent, in this Morristown orchard, heaving apples towards the doe, with you, to end something here with this kissing and this tacitly fiducial understanding that this finality has all the taut resilience of a trampoline lofting us back next time across the flat lasagna pans that our separate individual lives have devolved towards . . . this monody of kissing—this flicker of emulsion.

The germs in her nostril clung from tiny hairs which bristled like stalactites, and she said "Ahhhhhhchooooooo!" And from her delicious mouth sallied forth bits of a cyclist moving from left to right, bits of blue body-warm linen, bits of a tattle, bits of sky —of its blue polyhedra, bits of a spritz.

—Gesundheit.

—Thanks.

"May I have this dance, senorita?"

"You are indeed a wonderful man, Captain Parker!"

—Thanks.

PERSONAL PAGE

Everyone throw your beach balls at Liz Fox.   Tonight? Liz Fox.   Someone said "Liz Fox has the copies."   Liz Fox arrived and left.   O.K., enough Liz Fox anecdotes! Liz Fox said "The thicket is covered with petrol."   Liz Fox had become a trembling oil spill.   Did you hear? Liz Fox wanted my recipe.   Someone's creating the "Liz Fox" look.   My family was huddled around the radio when Liz Fox said, "Today will live in infamy."   Liz Fox had a magazine and walked a crooked mile.   Liz Fox is a notorious terrorist with international extortion never far from her thoughts.   This is the first edition of Liz Fox.   Liz Fox moved her tomato plants away from the window to keep them from freezing.   "They're cleaning Liz Fox up" was in the news.   Can't you find Liz Fox's name in the white pages, foreign student?   Standing at the far end of his yellow station-wagon, Liz Fox felt sad again.   Liz Fox lost her baby and couldn't let go but it was just her soap opera that was on.   That guy fitted Liz Fox for gauntleted gloves. Liz Fox demanded that they reopen the investigation of the Attica massacre.   Some guys smoked about a gram of really fine Liz Fox while they listened to records.   Everyone followed Liz Fox to the out-of-the-way restaurant. Dance Liz Fox. Go! Go! Go! Go! Go! Rip your wig off! Liz Fox said "Tomorrow will be better than today was!"

"LA VIDA"

Who's your father? See that over there, he said, pointing to a fifteen year old smoking a cigarette. Him. That's my mother, he said, pointing to a pudgy guy in a fedora. You want your shot or not, he asked. Definitely, I said, I've been planning this trip to Europe for over three years. Well, he said, take your pants off and lie on those newspapers. As soon as the needle's in you'll be in Europe. He sang. Left a good job in the city. Workin for the man every night and day. Smallpox killed near everyone round here, reckon. I could hardly sputter a few words of thanks when the hay wagon jerked forward and we were off again. What are those, I asked, pointing to a cluster of make-shift tents near the high school. The teenagers who've left home live there. They still go to high school? I asked. Oh yes they like school very much because all their friends are there. I jumped out and ran to the front of the school. There was a tall beautiful oriental girl. She reached under her shirt, unfastened her bra, and put it around her waist like a belt. I followed her, along with another couple who'd been standing nearby, into one of the tents. I sat in the corner with the oriental girl and she cleaned some grass. The other couple was on the ground, kissing and clutching at each other. Then this happy-go-lucky guy came in and sat down with me and the oriental girl. The girl who was kissing the boy worked his pants off and tugged at his boxer shorts moaning. The boy grabbed at the tent's flap trying to close it all the way. She wriggled out of her pants she wore no underwear. Suddenly the happy-go-lucky guy dropped his pants jumped up and entered her from behind. I'll never forget her expression of surprise and pleasure as she arched her back and said ah ah ah!

PANGS IN THE P.M.

"My son's name was Diablito Leyner. Diablito — 'little devil.' At three years of age he was five-seven, had body hair, a deep voice, read books, danced when you took him to Isadora's, used stick deodorant, had sex with people's housemates, had a receding hairline, drank too much now and then, and worried about things constantly. In fact, he was almost identically like myself. He was conceived on a spring night in a first floor alcove of the geology building where I'd found a janitress stooped in front of a display case of quartz specimens, completely transfixed with an annular sample of lapis lazuli. I tip-toed in back of her, lifted her skirt up, and we mated. So, one day I was defrosting my freezer. I'd put two or three bags of frozen vegetables in the back of the toilet tank to keep them cool. Diablito approached me from behind with a copy of Paradise Lost and read a passage: 'O foul descent! that I who erst contended / With Gods to sit the highest, am now constrain'd / Into a Beast, and mixt with bestial slime...' I stopped hacking away at the ice and told him it was time he hit the road and find out where he was at. 'Take a bag of peas,' I said, 'and remember—eat where the truckdrivers stop, the food's bound to be good.' That was the last I ever saw of him. He's changed his name to Richard Finestein. And he's failed in half a dozen business ventures. The stock market, real estate, retail clothing, insurance, you name it. People say 'Richard Finestein—he's got a magic wand up his ass—everything he touches turns to shit.' Well, I'm not the kind of guy who blubbers over spilled milk, if you know what I mean—but for weeks I'd just sit in that dilapidated Boston rocker and sweat buckshot and dumdum bullets and every night at the same time, a bus passed under my window followed, three minutes later, by a harried little man running with an overnight bag. Every night. You could time an egg by it. He'd run a few blocks and then stop, take a deep breath, turn around and walk back. One night I couldn't contain myself—I flew downstairs just in time to collar the guy as he rushed by. 'You again!' he raged, 'Every night you make me miss my bus!' And he broke my grasp and ran, as was wonted, a few blocks, stopped, took a deep breath, turned around and walked back. As he approached me, he tipped his hat and bowed, 'Excuse my behavior before,' he said, 'but I was in a terrible rush,' and walked away... and I'm left standing there and I'm thinking—I'm like the guy who's rummaged through a ton of glazed popcorn for something to hock and comes up with nothing but a sticky hand—and I'm thinking—what the fuck am I doing—I'm an asshole... and I was drinking so much V-8 juice that I always had diarrhea and I couldn't find a razor I liked—the twin blades would get jammed up with hair and the little disposable single blades would cut me to ribbons..."

"Mark... Mark... Mark," Barbara said, "like, what's really bothering you?"

That department store signal was in my head—Ping Ping   Ping   Ping.

"Aaaaaaaw Barbara... I may have killed two or three Tai Chi students with that Datsun of mine."

"You could use some more tea. Say when." she said, bending at the waist and pouring more hot water into the cup that shook in my trembling hand. Her breasts fell forward against the printed calico of her blouse. But even this movement seemed alien and incidental as did the movement of the drapes that seemed to inhale and exhale in the breeze through the open living room windows, as did the sound of the plastic knobs at the end of the drapery cords bouncing against the wall, as did the sensation of scalded flesh as tea spilled over the top of my cup onto my hand.

"When." I said.

"Is Joe Safdie's head loose?" Barb asked.

"No Barb," I said, "he just waves his head around that way when he talks—it's just a habit."

"Is it attractive?"

"I don't know, Barb—you'll have to ask another girl that question."

"Well tell me how it happened."

"It's just a mannerism that someone develops...an idiosyncrasy."

"Mark...Mark...Mark...Not that. How did the accident, that you may have had, happen?"

"Aaaaaaaaaw Barbara...."

Then the phone rang. It was Lisa.

"I can't talk now. I'm in the shower. Bye."

"Aaaaaaaaaaaw Barbara.... It was between Cascade and Baseline. I was on my way to Chautauqua. They move so slowly. They crossed the street so slowly."

"Did you kill em? Did you kill em?" she asked and her eyes got real big.

"I don't know. They move so slowly it's hard to tell if they're dead or alive."

"There'd be dents in your car if you hit anyone." Barbara said, blending some soy sauce into a bowl of mayonaisse with a wicker-handled whisk.

"I don't know. They're very thin—like sparrows—almost not there—with awful anorexic pallors. They'd fall like candle-pins."

From the window I could see my Datsun. And I could see the balled-up mimeographed sheets that teased and capered about its full tires. I kept a megaphone near the window so that in case a youth leaned on the hood or set a milk dud on the windshield and poised his fist above, I could broadcast my vehement anger below and watch him flee. The car was, after all, my responsibility. From the window, I could see the Flatirons, not quite piebald with snow and rock and not quite hypertrophically lush with green growth—but in between. I used to stand on the balcony and watch the setting sun imbrue the sky with its puce and blue-indigo stains and then fall down, deep in the Rockies where it would rattle around in the night like a black roulette ball. Then I'd go back inside and watch the news. Then maybe make chopped-meat and Rice-a-Roni, then have coffee. Then later take a glossy girl from the stack, from my seraglio of magazines, and rock against the cool sheets in a cool sweat and fall asleep before I could even mess.

"There'd be blood on your car if you hit anyone." Barbara said.

"What?"

"There'd be blood on your car if you hit anyone."

"I don't know. I think I went right to a car wash. And then I went to Baseline Liquors."

"What happened there?"

"The guy there said 'How ya doing today?' and I said 'I can't believe how much beer costs' and he said 'It's really something' and I asked 'Does it just keep going up all the time or what?' and he said 'Every time they bring the fuckin stuff in —it's gone up...'"

"Wait a second," Barbara said.

"What?"

"Nothing. Go on."

"And then I said 'It's always because something else from somewhere else is costing someone else more,' and he said 'The big companies got their heads together on this thing,' and I said 'The oil companies sure do' and he reached over the counter and grabbed my lips and pulled them apart so that all my gums were showing and I had him shred one of those free entertainment guides across my teeth and with two of the shreds, I demonstrated how asymptotic lines and hyperbolae never meet and I said that this also shows why Mendel, the Austrian botanist, and Joe Tex, the American singer, would never meet—and then he began to weep. 'What is it?' I asked 'I'm weeping,' he said, 'because I'm sad that Mendel and Joe Tex will never meet.' "

"That asymptotic line business was a mean trick," Barbara said.

"I know. But anyway—then, for some reason, I told him that he wasn't like an M&M—that he'd melt in my mouth *and* in my hands."

"Did he yell at you? Did he chase you out?" Barbara asked.

I looked at her. "Why do you cover your neck. It's either covered with your hair or you wear turtle-necks. Why don't you either wear your hair up in buns or gathered, at least, in braids or ponytails and not wear turtle-necks."

"Those . . . are your ideas," she said bitterly.

I decided to consult a hypnotist in order to find out exactly what had happened. I picked one out of the yellow pages. He was located on Canyon Boulevard. He took me back into his apartment which he apparently used as his office. It was a mess.

"Before I got into hypnosis," he said, "I used to run the Boulder Institute of Balneology. The science of baths. Everyone specializes these days. There aren't any general balneologists anymore."

"What was your specialty?" I asked.

"Cyst soaking."

Then he said "Let's get down to business."

I inquired as to his methods.

"My method's one of the latest. What I'm going to have you do, Mark, is to wash dishes until you fall into a trance," he said, pointing to a sink full of dirty skillets, and saucepans and utensils, "If that doesn't work we'll have you vacuum and dust and do some laundry until the trance is achieved."

"Well," I said, "let's get going."

Two hours later, I'd cleaned the whole kitchen, made the beds, shampooed the rugs and straightened the book shelves and magazine racks.

"Well," I asked, "what did I say?"

"Mark," he said, plucking the check from my hand, "we've found that relating to the patient the details of what he's said under hypnosis is generally contraindicated. Have a nice day."

"You too." I said.

When I got back to the apartment, Barbara was at the stove.

"I haven't read about anyone being killed," she said.

"How could you have —we never see a newspaper around here."

"Well, we would've heard."

"I think I heard about it —I think I heard one of the Tai Chi people talking —he said 'Because of these murders, the whole Tai Chi community is very tense. And we hate being tense. And we hate ourselves for hating something. And we can't stand the anxiety that brews in the self-hatred. So we're all really unbalanced.' And then they asked him what games Tai Chi people like to play with their kids when they get bored in the car on long trips —and he said, spotting the most license plates from a particular state, or naming state capitals, or the animal-mineral-vegetable game. Then he said, 'Once, a Tai Chi person hit a toll attendant in the forehead with a quarter because he thought it was one of those change receptacles. We think that's a funny story —and when we think something's funny —we laugh.' "

Then the phone rang. It was Lisa.

"I can't talk —I'm in the middle of shaving. Bye."

Barbara started to tickle me. "Don't," I giggled. "I'll keep doing it if you laugh." I couldn't stop laughing though—so she wouldn't stop tickling me. I was in convulsions. At one point, she tickled me so well that my body had a great spasm and my head crashed through the television screen. Everyone was in there.

"I gotta get out of here for awhile," I said, "while I'm gone I wonder if you could do that seam on my blue corduroy jacket."

I kept trying to fly to the District of Columbia. But each time, the plane would take off from Denver, fly for four hours or so and then land in Denver—and the passengers would get up and stretch and reach into the overhead luggage compartments for their coats, queue up and deplane, as if we'd really arrived in the District of Columbia after all. But I doubt we ever had.

Each day I'd watch the newspaper boy arrive at my apartment and stand in the center of the complex's vast atrium and toss the papers up towards the second and third floor balconies. But he could never reach the apartments and the papers would just fall back to the ground. And he'd throw them again and they'd fall short again. Then he'd throw them with more force and they'd land on the roof. Then he'd throw them a little softer and they'd hit the balcony's railing and tumble back to the ground. Then much much harder and they'd fly over the roof. And finally he'd leave, not having delivered a single paper. So tenants were held virtually incommunicado from the world and not infrequently there'd be screams from apartment windows "Is it baseball season or basketball?!"

Another week began on the radio. Air blew through the heat vent and someone in an adjoining apartment was using their garbage disposal. These were things I noticed. Because in many ways I lived with my apartment and not in it, I knew its moods and habits. I thought the apartment was so horny. I looked for its diary everywhere. It must have longed for something as neuter and clean as it was. Within its confines, I could smell myself and vent in the inexpressible ways an unexpurgated hatred of the other women I wanted desperately desperately to just hold me and kiss me—that would be better than fucking—just being held. A friend lent me his guitar and one night I just played Under The Boardwalk. Under The Boardwalk   Under The Boardwalk   Under The Boardwalk "On a blanket with my baby. . ." These were the feelings I held. The walls of the apartment were covered with lipstick marks of big inhuman kisses. The next morning I woke up and began to live more realistically. I ate breakfast quickly and put my sweat pants and orange sweat shirt on and drove to the basketball courts at the Williams Village dormitories. As I entered the court, there was an almost unprecedented ovation and I sang the Everly Brothers' "never knew what I missed until I kissed ya" as I dribbled. It was there, I think, at mid-court, beneath the clouds' pink under-bellies, that I decided that the most prudent and expedient thing I could do was leave Boulder.

I made up my mind not only to relocate but to assume a new identity. To weather the future under cover. To lose myself in the great anonymity of the mid-west. I applied to an exchange program that would place me with a mid-western farming family. And with greater dispatch than I could have hoped for, I received notification that I'd been accepted and that I was to join my new family at the first opportunity. The speed with which my application was processed was due, I think, to the unassailable discretion with which I'd answered the application's queries. Where it asked why I wanted to live with a farm family, I wrote, "Because I like farmers." Where it asked why I liked farmers, I put, "First the farmers angered Washington residents by trampling the mall and driving their tractors into the reflecting pools, but then really charmed them by plowing capital motorists out from under that uncharacteristically heavy snowfall. And some farmers even sought a brief respite from controversy beneath snowy monuments and dashed off impassioned letters to wives and sweethearts." And on the part of the application where it asked what kind of letters the farmers sent, I put: "Dear Helen, If you got telephone cable and wrapped it around all the planets and stars so that if you wanted to you could call other galaxies and universes you would not speak to a finer prettier best-cookinest gal than you are Helen. I mean it too, brown eyes."

Needless to say, I was delighted at the sudden prospect of being able to live quietly, and without constant foreboding.

I called my friend Bianca and invited her to the Boulderado for a drink. It's funny, y'know I even remember what we had —she drank Spanish coffee and I had bourbon and soda. And while we were drinking, the waiter brought a telephone over, "It's for you, sir." It was Lisa.

"I can't talk now," I said, "I'm insulating. I've got fiberglass all over me. Bye." I hung up and called Barbara.

"Listen Barbara, I'm having a drink with Bianca at the Boulderado. Call up the airline and make a reservation for me."

"Forget it," she said, "If it's so important to have a drink with Bianca, let her make your calls."

"Look Barb, do as I say or I'll read *your* letters to a room full of English 119 students."

When I got back to the apartment, Barbara was on the floor, filling a syringe with soy sauce and mayonaisse. She clenched and unclenched her fist a few times, looped her belt around her arm and pulled it tight with her teeth.

I could see the words at the bottom of the glass I'd been drinking from.

Barbara turned to me, "There are cops in the kitchen."

There were four cops disguised as three cops. One cop was part wasp, part fascist pederast. One cop was short and fat. One cop was drenched in Aqua Velva. They were in my kitchen.

My heart hit the linoleum like a clump of dough, with a real bottom of the ninth splat that evaporated into a cloud of valerian vapor, a real gaseous calm, a real back-to-mom, a real relieved throb. Cause being caught for the wrong thing is the loftiest exoneration there is. And maybe they got me for stealing cigarettes from King Soopers, or stealing books from Brillig Works, or reading other people's letters in the mail room, or stealing newspapers from other apartment complexes, or lying without let-up, lying about the woman I love without question so other women will sleep with me, or napping when most of the citizenry is slaving away, or keeping my sea-onion in the closet or overbreading my chicken or being myopic and algophobic and predatory.

"Big deal," I said. "Big shit. What's the big fuss all about," I said, as they led me outside to the car.

I stopped walking and tilted back my head and for a minute just felt the rain fall on my face and for just a second it felt like being very young again . . . another little kid who'd skated in his dress shoes across the frozen ponds that had formed on the settlement's big plans, for a big future, for big thinkers, with big wallets, on big behinds.

"Asshole." I said.

Taken off the face of the earth.

From its static electricity and unctuous detergents.

"Face of the earth!" I swore.

I swore at the crowd of things I knew.

And someone yelled from a window, "Is it hockey season or baseball?"

"Asshole season," I said, "Asshole season."

HISTORICAL PLAYS:

Sides A and B

A

DISCO DIASPORA

WAITRESS: Sir, I'm sorry but we're out of Thousand Island. You can have French, Blue Cheese, Russian, or the house vinaigrette.

IRTZY: Alright . . . French. (Then hissing to himself.) Oh bold stalk of enmity. Phototropic tattersall of crimson and black. Lopped far above root by the blunted edge of compromise's loose desultory scythe! You shall stretch forth again. And nourish the air with fragrant revenge!

LEIBMAN: Your stalk, sahib, is still redolent of that wench's soiled hole.

IRTZY: That is no wench, Leibman, that is my dear wife.

(Enter IRTZY's wife, MUE)

IRTZY: What bulletin do you bear, faithful partner?

MUE: Only this, dearest.

IRTZY: What?

MUE: This.

IRTZY: What do you mean this? This what?

MUE: The Hebrews, and that means me and you, are dispersing to a heavy beat.

IRTZY: Like what beat, you thing.

MUE: Just snap your fingers and get it, get to it. Get it to it. Uh shma yip uhh yich yisro ya yaka!!!!

(Exeunt)

B

I LOVE (TO FEEL YOUR LOVE)

VOICES FROM THE CROWD: He doesn't take the static concept of time seriously!
He's hyper-heroic!
He's like menacingly good-looking!

ENVOY: You are loved by my country's people, Mr. Premier.

TRANSLATOR: "Bilos derung zha afshler biobnz, Di. Premebnz."

PREMIER (nodding and smiling): Er vagator ma wot; af gevunt ben hadis menoritz gool $\overline{aa}$ pen sodrana helopants banistrosa eeko vantrick al put, shen so glisso va lamotor ben mu fak. Hhaa... Hho hho!

TRANSLATOR: "This makes me warm; there are those in my country's neighboring regions who would decorate me not with laurels and medals of valor, but with a tight noose around my throat. Haa... Ho ho!"

(A massive asteroid collides with Earth.)

CROWD:
ENVOY: Aaaaaaaaah!

TRANSLATOR: "Yaaaaaaaah!"

PREMIER: Yaaaaaaaah! Yaaaaaaaah! Yaaaaaaaah!

(Fade)

THE RIVER

Look in my closet. There is a blue double-breasted blazer with gold buttons. It is the afternoon and someone is watching us from their sofa and eating cheez doodles. O.K.? Do you hear the anvil falling from the sky and striking you on the head? Now you're an accordion. I'm putting on my blazer and I'm skipping along the river bank, playing a polka on you. The crippled mice are tossing away their crutches and dancing behind me! The cute mouse women are screaming and fainting. But someone with a big vacuum cleaner is chasing us, and sucking the mice up. There goes the last one! Thup! Now I'm sitting alone on the edge of the river in my blue blazer, and you're an accordion. Assume your old shape and let's go for a drive in my motorboat, or else we will die.

THE BOAT SHOW

Look. I've just returned from a used bookstore. It's run on the honor system. You pay at the main store across the street. It's easy to steal the books. There are economics textbooks, volumes of Shakespeare filled with sophomoric underlining and marginalia, books that people probably purchased in drugstores and supermarkets before going on vacation, marriage manuals, and stacks and stacks of National Geographics. That's clear, isn't it? I've given a partial list in order to generally characterize the store's stock. Once I stole an art magazine from the place. I felt guilty. After all, it's commendable that someone has faith in other people these days, and it's commendable that someone is offering books at such cheap prices. More people should read, right? So this time I didn't steal anything. I simply went through a few piles of Modern Photography magazines and ripped out all the photographs of nude women I could find. When I got home, I tacked them up to the walls of my study. Are you following me so far? Now I am looking out the window of my study. I am going to try to make you see what I see. With me? O.K. A red car just drove by. A blue one. And then a white coupe with a black vinyl roof. A man in a white v-neck undershirt just leaned out his door and took his mail out of the box. His house is painted a kind of olive-green color. The house to the right of his is a very muted salmon-pink. The house to the right of that is a deep scarlet with white trim. Now, what color is the house next to that? I'll give you a minute or two. While you think, I'll have a cigarette and look at my new photographs. There's one of a blond woman I particularly like. She looks like a girl named Sharon I knew in Boulder. I think Sharon's married now and lives up in Buffalo, New York. Anyway...O.K., time's up. How many of you wrote down, red brick with beige trim? Good. Alright, now you've got the hang of it. Again, I'm going to try to make you sense what I sense. Ready? Here we go. The electric heater in my study runs on a thermostat. So all day it turns itself on and off. Sometimes, though, it gets too hot. Let's say it's getting too hot now. Follow me? I'm taking off my flannel shirt. O.K. O.K. I'll take off my undershirt too. Now I'm bare-chested. And for the sake of argument, I'll tack a spare photograph of two nudes on horseback to my chest. Ouch... there. Nice horse, huh? Now I'm looking out the window. A dog is howling. Awwwooooo. Awwwoooooooo. I hear a helicopter. I lean next to the window and check the sky. Very gray. A guy with a trainman's cap and ponytail just got out of a pick-up truck and walked up the street carrying a clipboard. Did you see him take the pen out from behind his ear? Good. A group of about fifteen African diplomats just walked by. If I didn't know better, I'd say one of them is pointing right at me. Look at all the litter in the street. That's terrible. Whatever happened to "keep American beautiful"? Went out with hula hoops and swallowing fish, right? O.K. Look at the beer cans. I can make out Stroh's, Miller, a Michelob...and a Budweiser. Now I'm going to look directly beneath my window. I'm going to try to be very specific here. Next to the curb are two plastic trash barrels, green and red with black lids. Adjacent to the trash barrels is the neighbor's hedge...it's made up of some kind of perennial shrub, (I'm squinting now and leaning way over), some kind of perennial shrub with prickly... prickly bipinnate leaves and tiny tiny pink flowers. You are enchanted by the tiny delicate pink petals. N'est-ce pas? You want to crush them with a mortar and pestle and massage them into your scalp. You are repeating the word ''pestle'' to yourself until it loses its meaning. Alright. Don't move. Do you see the reflection of my finger in the window? Do you see the reflection of my face? Am I pointing to a dimple, a pock mark, or a dueling scar? Yell out your answer! Now we are dancing. Are you inhaling as I exhale? In other words, have our gears meshed? Are you still lashed to the cross of my thoughts? Uh oh. I'm feeling light-headed. The right side of my brain is giving a blow job to the left side. You don't get a choice on this one —I'm going to do all four —I'm going to a. Smash my china to the music of Felix Mendelssohn, b. Drive the endless highway west, c. Collect the latex footprints that lead to this room, *and* d. Open my veins in a warm bath. Now where is my tweed jacket with a wedding band in every pocket? Where is my yiddish phrase book? My itinerary? That's the last one. You'll have to leave. I'm going to throw myself out the window. Put me in one of the plastic trash barrels. Tack a photograph of yourself to my forehead. Goodbye now. We part!

PROSE POEM/
A JOKE FOR GINGER

The exposition's lights are pale and diffuse through the condensation, the trolley cables and pylons are lightly dusted with snow outside the big shed, downtown St. Louis, the mechanical chicken scuttles off the cutting board and the thread of gold at her ankle throws light off its turning key. The snowy streets record the trails of unnaturally bulky particles that splinter and fuse in millionths of seconds though, elsewhere, and more indigenous to this version, his prints lead to the door of a household, that he opens. "Ooooooh," she shivers, "this earth shuttle is lonely." "Pass over that bottle of Sniggering Walter," he says, "Daddy's home." Mental months spire into the air and swerve as if pulled by the oven fan. It's hard to forget this scene that plays and replays so often. He goes and sits at the piano and she follows and stands behind him with her arms around his neck. And they sway together as he plays. Dinner burns, giving off a warm ocher glow. In one version the woman is someone I know. In another version their bodies look like decoupage-covered wood. And although in some versions the piano is electric and they're literally bottomless, the only one with a provocative conclusion is the version in which they affiliate themselves with a community theater's production of *Special Yearnings* which ends with the fiery crash of a red convertible that in turn detonates a domino chain of underground nuclear reactors from St. Louis to Worcester, Mass. And in this version, I'm visiting someone in Worcester and I'm too blasted to make love, so I find a station I like on the radio and go lie on the rug. Get it, Ginger? Too blasted.

KING PLEASURE'S MOOD/
A FABLE FOR LAURA

The guy smoking the cigar used to be a stunt man, sunlight glaring off the missile's warhead, as he slips an assortment of pamphlets about cryonics into his wife's purse. The town had just instituted a pee-wee football league. He had to drop junior off every Sat. afternoon, 1:30. The field was ten minutes away and the car had to pass the community pool's parking lot—the side with the basketball hoops. Even the Russians knew his route. His daughter rides on top of the car, straddling the hood, with white vinyl boots on and a men's thermal undershirt as tight as skin, she has no breasts yet, her nipples are dark wide ovals. At home, his wife draws a bath. The mirror fogs. She tests the water with her foot. They'd lived in the house for almost a year. For years before that, a For Sale sign remained jabbed in the hedge. The missile scared off prospective buyers. "That thing," they'd grimace, turning on their heels. Walter waited in the bushes by the hoops, loosening up his wrists and readjusting his grip on the rope. As the car passed, he lassoed the daughter. And reeled her into the shrubbery. "What's this about?" she coughed. "King Pleasure's in one of his moods," he said. She curtseys. "King Pleasure.... it's a pleasure to make your acquaintance," she says, blushing. "I'm sick of the dehydrated pussy all my available girlfriends offer," he says, stamping his feet. "Sing this:" she says, "Don't think about the future / don't think about the used to be / here's a feeling that's growing / feed it orally... you fool." He kisses her. "You're too young for any more sex," he explains. He pats her head. "When I used to see you on top of that car, I thought you were older." "I'm old enough! You wanna see?" she whines. Her expression is sullen. "See what?" Walter asks. "Follow me" she says, slipping the rope off her waist, emerging from the bushes onto the street. She takes him home. The walk takes about twenty-five minutes. When they arrive she leads him into the backyard, putting a finger to her lips as she relatches the gate behind her. "Shhhh ...quiet, my mother's still home." She gets a lawn chair from the shed and unfolds it for him, "Watch." She walks up to the missile, opens a panel, tinkers with something and dives behind a mound. With an ear-splitting howl and a dense circle of white flame at its base, the missile begins to climb. It lifts slowly at first, rising above the roofs, tree tops, and telephone poles. And then it seems to accelerate at a more severe angle and, in a matter of two minutes or so, disappears from sight. She's crying hysterically, ripping at her hair, kicking clumps of dirt and grass out of the ground. "See what you made me do?!" she wails. Walter feels sick now. "Me and my moods..." he mutters.

UNTITLED/
A LULLABY FOR SHARON

The anonymous citizens of Targetgrad conduct business as usual: the saxophone student with overbitten embouchure squeaks throughout the early P.M. & I'd rather be with you in the fields of meadow mushroom and sundew where antelopes in sapphire blue satin regimentals slide on their asses across the unrestricted downgrades —jews can play there—did you remember to bring the Bloomingdale's bag with the box of marzipan fruits that I, and don't ask me why, bought for judy —there're ants getting in my boiled picnic lunch! —Quiet. Quiet! I thought I heard something funny. Funny ha-ha like Joan Rivers? —Quiet! Shhhhhh! Like a jump rope cutting through the air. Like a tea-kettle whistling on a distant stove. Like a wheezing daughter coming to me. It's chillier. Quieter. Maybe dustier. Where will you tell me you were? Now how do I put you at ease at this conjectured distance? Dark clouds with cartridge bandoliers slung across their chests escort the sun to its remote place. Now how do I smooth your hair, or refold the sheet under your chin, or pour the inky ointment from that unmarked vial in a river between your breasts and yodel and beat my chest and swing from a vine and share a cigarette with you and twirl the revolver around my finger and cajole you into shutting your eyes, and sleeping through the racket this'll make? Undoubtedly you are somewhere dining with a gentle-man of considerable means. His head is as sparse of hair as an insect's. Picturing spittle at his lips is no problem. You ask someone at an adjoining table where a phone is. They direct you. You dial my number. I answer and proceed as rehearsed. Sleep, I say, shut your eyes and shut everything but tranquillity from your mind and, if possible, wake me up tomorrow. It'll be early, I know, barely after dawn. I'll drag myself out of bed, look out of the window, see the snow and say, well, judging from the looks of things outside, I guess I'll take a train to the today factory. Now, farewell. From my vantage point, in this fusty room, on this stiff carpet, watching the battle-ax and pike rattle against the wall, discerning that sound's approach, farewell, farewell. Tonight will be a false bottom. The water you gulp down will taste like a mountebank's elixir. In the corner of the sky, his necktie glows like a filament. The trees are momentarily flamboyant.

THE SPIN CYCLE

Everything I love is gone.
The blue jay hops
from Corinthian column to Corinthian column,
alternately aphasiac and wildly logorrheic.
My hands are meaty like two catcher's mitts.

Your nose is bleeding into the plastic dish of meow mix
like a leaking faucet in a mobile home where
he is eating a baked potato with chives and sour cream,
the liver of a blaspheming jew, a salad of pistils and stamens,
and the bicycle seat on which you'd ridden to grandmother's
    house.

The fishermen serenade their Juliets, adrift in listing dinghies, and the tall trees undulate in the rain like thick inky manes of hair. I am speaking a language called There's Gold In Them Thar Hills. You are speaking a language called She Feels Like Buttering The Palm Of His Hand And Frying It.

A is for an anonymous man, chasing bubbles of your saliva through the forest with a slingshot made from the elastic waistband of his jockey shorts. B is for Brenda, waving to the peculiar foil ships which flicker against the sky like yahrzeit candles. C is for Gianni Clerici, the flamboyant columnist for Jerusalem's irresponsible tabloid, Il Giorno, his windshield dappled with the ocher and burgundy leaves of autumn.

There is a lake for lovers only, called He'd Known Janet In Delaware When She Was A Super-Realist Painter With Freckled Breasts, and rising from the lake is a spectacular monolith that makes the Statue of Liberty look like an anorexic Barbie doll, and from a window in its bronze bouffant I can see you through my telescope, whispering into the ear of another man.

In the moonlight, in your sheer camisole, in your cadaverous eyeshadow, you wind your Timex, and call him the best fuck in Jerusalem. You call his mouth Hans. You call his chest Jan. You call his penis Inspector Soto. You call his buttocks Officer Shange and the Prosecutor Nickie DuBois.

Ahmed and his ugly daughter are playing catch with a boneless chuck steak. She's making a sound like boom lakka lakka lakka boom lakka lakka lakka.

I am the chattering wooden teeth of the president who never told a lie in the crooked mouth of the president who never spoke the truth, and you are the sound of a match striking the unshaven chin of a cowboy, you are the sound of a harmonica falling from a tree and hitting me on the head as I stretch my penis like a bungee cord, chianti-sodden and disconsolate.

The Scarsdale Diet is dead.
Give me a t-shirt the color of azalea
and call Deng Xiaoping, Chapstick Xiaoping.

The industrial countryside vibrates powerfully beneath our sleeping bags and hibachis. Like voltage, "csók" (the Magyar word for kiss) passes from Gabor sister to Gabor sister to Gabor sister. But why do we plunge our faces into vats of formaldehyde like half-witted marines and allow these ghosts, however Rubenesque, to rifle through our luggage and filch our implements of happiness, our insect repellant, our tinker toys, our spanish fly, and puerto rican rum? Is it because, in the diffuse moonlight, this coppice of barbershop poles resembles the magnificent Piazza di Spagna; and, unable to articulate our loneliness, we belch like prehistoric animals and count our remaining days on the fingers of a single hand . . .

Distant tom-toms herald the approach of bedtime,
and you, "drows'd with the fume of poppies,"
sleep the sleep of enormous emu.

How I long to give you one last csók.
But now you are far away.

And here I waste,
sequestered deep in the forgettable mountains
of my ancestral homeland.